Bitter Sweet

52 STORIES

Heidi Hansen

H3 Press
2019

First Printing October 2019

ISBN: 978-0998252674

Cover design by Alan Halfhill

Published by:
H3 Press, PO Box 312, Carlsborg, WA 98324
H3Press@olypen.com

DEDICATION

I dedicate this book to all those who have influenced and guided my writing: to my father for his love of words and a good pun, to my writing groups which keep me putting pen to paper, and to my husband for his technical skill and support.

Contents

FRIDAY NIGHT FIGHTS

Long before there were Fight Clubs, my dad would tune the television to the Friday Night Fights. We were lucky enough to have a TV set, but only one, which meant you watched what dad wanted. And Friday nights it was boxing. I don't know why he chose that; it didn't seem to match his white-collar career or calm manner.

I hadn't thought about it in years, but because I watched with him, I knew that Muhammad Ali was known before as Cassius Clay. I remember him dancing in the ring, with his lyrical rhymes.

Now Friday nights have a different zing. Everyone in this northern Wisconsin town crams into the Moose Lodge for the all you can eat fish fry. The management stopped taking reservations years ago, so if you don't get there and line up before five, it can take you hours to get inside. The police were called last Friday, and they shut the place down. I was standing outside lined up nice and orderly when the squad cars arrived, lights flashing, sirens screaming. Everyone started elbowing each other trying to see inside.

No one knew what was happening. Someone shouted they heard gunfire, another thought he smelled smoke. The officers, suited up in their riot gear, were mustering at the entrance. Then an officer yelled to "clear the area." I thought fists would fly over losing their place in line, but everyone seemed compliant until another officer said, "Go home, we're shutting it down."

You'd have thought these were starving people the way they moaned and groaned, and me among them. But once you get the idea of the fish fry in your head, you can't let it go. We backed up a good ten feet but kept our line intact. One or two resigned their places and headed to their cars. Most of us still wanted a chance at the fish fry but speculating about the reason the police were called was a close second.

When the police were assembled, they opened the double doors and flooded in like a river going over its banks. They barked out orders and you could hear the diners inside screaming. Several diners with their bibs still tucked into their collars, sprinted out the door headed to the parking lot. It was obvious they were fleeing the scene, and I elbowed Bobby who's my second or third cousin. "I bet they didn't pay."

He nodded back and I could see him making a mental note to try that someday.

That's when we saw my ex-husband's brother, Fat Roy, come out. I yelled at him to come over. He held a plate piled high with fried fish and French fries, ketchup on his chin.

"What's happening in there?" I asked.

"Ho boy," he said. "Some kinda' food fight."

"What did you see? Who called the police?"

He laughed. "You remember that man who used to run the gas station over by the Walmart?"

"You mean Davey something or other. Old man?"

"Yep, that's the one. Said they shut down the gas

station 'cuz he was scaring away the ladies with his thing always hanging out, 'cuz, his fly was open. Well he's at the buffet and there's only one crab leg left." Fat Roy picked up one of his fish pieces and looked it over before popping it into his mouth.

"And what happened?" Cousin Bobby asked.

"Hey Bobby," Fat Roy said. "I didn't see you there. Well, Davey takes the tongs and goes in for the one crab leg, and this other pair of tongs grabs the crab leg from him. He's screaming that it's his and to let go."

"Who'd you say was the other person?"

"That's the damnedest thing, Bobby, it was your momma."

"She was supposed to save places for us in line," Bobby said to me.

I shook my head, "And that was enough for somebody to call the cops?"

"Oh that weren't but the start of it. They're both pulling on that crab leg with the tongs, then the crab leg fell to the floor. Davey started hitting Bobby's mama with his tongs. Bobby's momma let go a juicy line of expletives and hit him back, then kicked at him. Davey backed up knocking into the table, causing a big ole' pot of bake beans to tipsy over onto the floor. Davey slipped and fell yelling, 'Looky what you did now.'"

"Lordy, lordy," Bobby said, "My momma's got a temper. Once she gets it up, you can't bring it down."

"That's when Bobby's mama picked up the bottle of ketchup and squirted it over poor Davey's head. He reached up onto the table and grabbed whatever he could. He got the bowl of cold slaw and threw it at her. She ducked. It went all over Mrs. Applegate."

"The mayor's wife!"

"I suppose that's when somebody called the police." He popped another piece of fish into his mouth.

"So that was it?"

"Hell no. It was a free for all from that point. The mayor grabbed a bowl of tartar sauce and poured it on your momma's head."

Bobby said, "Judas Priest, that must've really got her mad."

"You betcha. I filled my plate from the other end of the buffet and got out of there. When the police stormed in, there must have been fifty people throwing food. It was a mess."

Bobby and I looked at each other. Then we saw the police coming out. The officers marched handcuffed people, leading them to the paddy wagon. They must have arrested fifty people, some young, some old. It was a lot. Bobby and I tried to see which one of the food-soaked people was his momma, but it was hard to tell.

The manager of the Moose Lodge came out. "Show's over. Everybody go home lessen you want to come in and help us clean up. We got floors, walls, tables and windows to clean."

Bobby said, "I better git home and wait for Momma to call. Hope she's cooled off by then."

"Next Friday then?" I called to Bobby.

THE LETTER

I'm writing to explain about my mother. Whenever she had a particularly bad day—she'd call us kids together to play a game.

"What game?" my brother Mike would ask.

"A TV game," she'd say. "A very special one."

By the time I was four, I knew exactly what was going to happen. I would help my siblings bring out the treasure chest. It was a cardboard box with "Lucky Strike" on one side. Mike and Debby colored it with their crayons to make it resemble a pirate's chest. We would bring it to the living room, and everyone would take their places.

In the box was a long red cape with a white fur collar, long white gloves, a gold crown with big red jewels, a bouquet of red plastic roses and a broken flashlight that had been altered to look like a microphone.

Lastly, all five kids would go through a box of colorful pictures we had cut out of magazines. These were to be the prizes. What five prizes would we pick today? There would be rewards if we picked things she really wanted that day.

Mike being the oldest always got to play the part of Jack Bailey and mom was always the contestant. Debby would sit down at the piano and begin to bang out her version of "Pomp and Circumstance." Mike took the microphone and shouted, "Who wants to be Queen for a day?" Then he exclaimed, "The judges agreed that Mrs. Marjorie Probst was indeed Queen for the Day."

Mom would come center stage and "ooh" and "my gracious me" and then crouch down so that Liz and I could wrap the red cape over her shoulders. Tommy brought the crown to Jack Bailey to put on the Queen. Debby played another round on the piano. Then Mike said in his best Jack Bailey voice, "And Mrs. Marjorie Probst wins today . . . ta da!" Each of us would present her with a cut-out advertisement for what we hoped she really wanted.

One time Mike gave her a matching washing machine and dryer, Debby always gave her the electric dishwasher because washing dishes was Debby's job. Tommy bowed down with a flourish and presented mom with "a brand new car." Liz gave mom a fur coat, even though we lived in Arkansas and nobody wore fur coats. I always gave her the same thing, the one thing I wanted more than anything else, a puppy.

"Thank you, thank you, thank you," she would say.

Then we would wait. What would she do next?

One time she sat there for a whole hour with a smile on her face. Another time she tossed down the red roses and said, "Okay, back to work." We liked it when she said, "That was fun, let's all go out for ice cream."

* * *

"Are you kidding me? You can't write about that. Not the Queen for a Day thing. Write about something else," Debby said reading over my shoulder.

"Why do you say that? It was a special time."

"Yeah, special like it shows how crazy she really was."

"I think it shows how important it was to her."

"And another thing, that wasn't fur on the red cape."

"It wasn't, what was it?"

"First off, the cape was an old bedsheet and the fur collar was three maxi pads taped to the sheet."

"But it looked like fur. Mom called it ermine."

"It was white with some black lines and circles drawn on it. I guess you might want to believe it. You were pretty young back then."

"When was the last time we played it?"

"It was when Mike was in high school, and mom wanted to "play TV" when he had friends over. Mike said, "No," real loud and scary. Mom started screaming. It wasn't long after that that she went away, and Aunt Erma came to live with us.

"And then Mike went off to college, you got married and I came to live with you. It was better than with Aunt Erma."

"Yeah, but Tommy and Liz were stuck there with her till they got out of school. I think that's why Liz got pregnant. Anything to get out of that house."

"Then mom came home."

"And oh my god did she throw a fit when she found out Queen for a Day was cancelled the week before she came home."

"I was sad because she was my mom…"

"Yeah, we all have that torn feeling between wanting to be the good kid to our mother and realizing that she was crazy as a loon.

"And then she went to Vegas."

"That was a pretty spectacular episode."

"Who knew she would do that?"

"I know. Jack Bailey got a restraining order against her and she got arrested. First there in Vegas, then again when she showed up at his house in Beverly Hills."

"She just wanted to be Queen for a Day."

"Look where that got her. Now her lawyer wants us to write letters to the court asking for leniency. I don't know what to say other than that she needs help. Mom asked me what happened to the treasure chest. I'm worried she wants to wear the cape and crown to court."

"So you don't think writing about how important that show was to her will help explain her obsession with Jack Bailey?"

"Hmmm, when you put it that way, it was always being played out while we were growing up. Maybe it is the right thing. Go ahead, finish the letter."

* * *

So Judge, please understand that for the eight years that the television show was on, it saved my mother's sanity—it gave her something to look forward to, some way out of the life she had, though there was no way she could make it from our backwoods little town in Arkansas to Los Angeles to be a contestant. At sixteen, she had a child, then another, and another and another till she had all five of us. None of her husbands stayed long enough to form a bond with his child. Until she married a man named Sam Jones. He was my father. He loved us all and was a good man, but he was struck down by a big semi that ran off the highway to avoid a dog. The driver lost control and plowed right through the hardware store where daddy worked. That's when mom started losing touch with reality. She just wanted one chance to be Queen for a Day.

So you see, when they let her come home from the mental hospital, it broke her that Queen for a Day had been cancelled. Then Tommy graduated, and they played Pomp and Circumstance and that blew her away because that was the Queen for a Day music. She left after that on her quest to talk Jack Bailey into one more show. Just for her.

Sincerely,

Jackee Bailey Jones

72 HOURS

Hockett Weston was a quiet man. I first met him working in the Accounting department where he formulated statistics from vast piles of data. It made my head spin trying to understand what the reports he typed up meant. Apparently he knew what he was doing and was always right. He was methodical and punctual; arriving to work early, and on finishing assignments.

One day he shared with me pictures from a recent vacation to the high desert of Colorado. After looking over the pictures I asked what he thought of the area. He shrugged in response to my questions. Later, he admitted to me that there was a seventy-two-hour period unaccounted for. He had no explanation. "It was Tuesday, then it was Friday," he said. After that vacation, he was never the same. He rarely was at his desk by nine, and somedays never came in, or called. He was reprimanded and ultimately fired.

I ran into him one day coming out of a fast food restaurant. It's a wonder I recognized him. He was never a fancy dresser, but always clean, his slacks and shirts well-pressed. This day he wore a wrinkled and soiled t-shirt and jeans. His hair was long and unkempt, and he reeked as if he hadn't bathed in a week.

"Are you all right?" I asked.

He nodded, a slight smile of recognition, and mumbled "hello." Then walked off.

What had happened to him? I wondered to co-workers, but no one seemed to care. I never had, but now I was caught up in the puzzle.

Sometime later, during an art event throughout the main street, I came upon a painting of a close-up view of Saturn as seen from one of its moons. I was struck by the realism of the painting though no one had ever been there to see what it looked like. I asked the artist who was bent over another planetary landscape in the making. "What led you to paint this?"

"I saw it in a dream," he said. He didn't look up from his work on the canvas. His brush dipped and dabbled and dipped again.

Later I brought a friend over to look at the picture. By then the second one was completed. It stood on an easel with a "wet paint" sign waving in the breeze.

"Oh my," my friend commented.

"See Saturn here," I said pointing to it.

"It seems so real," she said.

It was then the artist turned toward me, and to my amazement, it was Hockett.

"Hockett? You're painting now?"

"Yes," he said.

"I never knew you were so talented." I blushed, embarrassed by my statement. I started to mumble but stopped because there was no way out of that. "I really like them."

"Thank you," he said.

"How much?" my friend asked. Would she really buy one of these paintings? She mumbled all afternoon that everything was overpriced.

"Sorry, they're not for sale."

"Why are you here, if not to sell your paintings?"

"I was asked to share in the day. No one said I had to sell them."

"But Hockett," I interjected, "you could get hundreds of dollars…"

"No!" he shouted, turning away. "Not for sale."

* * *

That was maybe twenty years ago. Today, The Daily News ran an article about a rented storage unit recently auctioned for non-payment. The winning bid of $200 bought the unknown contents. When they opened the unit, they found more than a hundred paintings, and the body of the expired artist. I almost missed that part of the story, but when they stated that the paintings were all of planetary landscapes, I knew what happened to Hockett.

The paintings were sold at auction to astronomers and scientists for hundreds of thousands of dollars because their landscapes matched the photographs now being relayed from orbiting telescopes.

Goosebumps sent shivers up my limbs. Where had he gone in Colorado? What revealed those visions to him?

AIRPLANES AND PAPER CLIPS

The magnetic container sat on the right side of my desk. I'd reach absently for a paper clip only to have all of them drag across my desk linked. "Keith," I would shout. He'd sit at his desk next door chuckling. Every day he did this to me. I'd either unlink them or get new ones from the supply cabinet only to have Keith link them up again.

I expected him to come in and innocently say "What?" and for a few minutes I waited.

Then the truth of the situation jerked me back to reality. Keith was a pilot, owned his own plane and was full of stories of his escapades. The airplane was World War II vintage and Keith had rebuilt or upgraded it from one end to the other. He towed it from one place to another behind his car with the wings taken off. Pretty funny to see that on the freeway.

Once he offered me a ride, and I accepted. An experienced flyer I was surprised by that flight in his two-seater plane over San Francisco Bay. I had no fear in a large 747 jet liner, but I had no experience in a small aircraft. As I stepped into the plane, I became aware of the close proximity of the ground. It would be easy to leave my right foot there on the tarmac, the other in the plane seemed fraught with risk. I swallowed that down and brought my foot into the plane hesitantly. I watched as the markers along the runway sped by, then up, up, up we went. This little metal can I was in could so easily be swatted down or simply fall from the sky. There was no hope of surviving such a crash.

Keith was an experienced and careful pilot. He told me all the things he was doing, checking the altimeter, watching the horizon, pointing to and explaining each dial and meter. He tapped one in the center console and it jiggled, then fell onto the floor. I gasped. He apologized and said it really wasn't important. My panic was palpable.

Around the bay, up toward Hayward, back across the salt flats to Fremont, then around the Alviso slough. We came back to the ground safely. I thanked him for the flight. He said, "See you tomorrow." We got into our respective cars and sped off in opposite directions on the 101.

A semi-truck crossed the line and took him. He died not in flight as he would have liked, though someone said it seemed the Chevy Vega did sail through the air for a moment.

ANOTHER CHANCE

What if you got another chance? Jack Van Dam wondered this as he walked along the pier on a particularly windy day. After a career of forty years as an accountant, he was forced to retire five years before, and recently dismissed from his volunteer position at the historical museum. It wasn't about the money. Ever since his wife died, he searched for purpose, and tried to make himself useful throughout the community.

Earlier that day, Jack had a chance encounter with a carnival barker. That's when he began to wonder if there was a chance to relive his life. Jack's memory of the event was dream-like. *Was it only a dream?*

What Jack remembered clearly, was the man. Slicked back dark hair, black suit, white shirt, red tie— too much of a stereotype to be anything but a dream. Jack found himself outside a tent, the carnival hawker called out, "Last Chance, Don't Miss This Opportunity." Jack stopped and listened, keeping his distance. The man locked eyes with him. Jack had no memory of making the decision to do so, but he felt compelled to put a twenty-dollar bill in the barker's hand and enter the tent.

The interior of the tent was colder than the afternoon air outside. A woman cackled somewhere in the distance. Something made the hairs on the back of his neck bristle. Jack turned to leave. The man in the suit blocked his way and closed the opening in the tent. He strode to the podium and in a booming voice welcomed them. A handful of folding chairs sat askew around the podium. Only two chairs were occupied, an older woman and a young man. Jack took the seat beside the young man.

Jack's memory of the details was hazy at best. "Another chance…An opportunity not to be missed…Fix something before the end. What memory plays over and over in your mind? What would you do differently if you had another chance?"

That was what Jack remembered. Hearing those words set in motion all sorts of thoughts. *My first love…What happened to Cathy? She said I fathered a child, but I never saw it… Was it a boy or a girl? Why didn't I make the time? I'd …*

The older woman sprang up crying. "I want to do it over, I need to fix it. Please." She fell to the man's feet, begging. He leaned down and said something to her. She threw her arms around him and thanked him. The man sitting beside Jack coughed loudly. Jack glanced at him, and when he looked back, the woman was gone. The man in the suit stood directly in front of Jack.

"What one event would you choose, Jack?" the man asked.

"Me?" Jack said, trying to reel in his thoughts.

"You have many memories. I see them. Pick one, just one. Jack, pick it now!"

Somewhere far off, Jack heard the plink of an electric guitar. That triggered another memory; the first time he heard Jimi Hendrix. He was so awe struck by the musician that he immediately chose his future as a guitarist. All summer he mowed lawns to make enough money to buy an electric guitar and an amp he saw in the local pawn shop. When he brought it home, his mother handed him headphones and told him, "No loud music." That summer, he hitched to see Hendrix in person several times. But he missed Woodstock. He was stuck in summer school, or he would have gone. He could mimic Hendrix chord for chord. He wanted to play with him. That had been his dream back then.

That was Jack's thought.

"Done," the man in the suit said.

"What?" Jack asked.

"You have thirty-six hours to bring a cashier's check for fifty thousand dollars to the address on this paper. Be on time." The man tucked a piece of paper into the right-hand pocket of Jack's coat.

"Fifty thou…?"

"You get this one chance Jack, or all that's left for you is the obituaries."

* * *

Jack stared down into his now cold coffee. *Was it a dream?* Jack pulled his coat tighter against the wind on the pier in Port Angeles. As he looked across the Strait of Juan de Fuca, his hand darted into the pocket. There was the piece of paper. Jack drew it out and read: "Elwha Bridge, two thirty a.m."

"What?"

He had no memory of agreeing to the meeting. A cold wind jostled him sideways. He crushed the paper in his hand and dropped it. The paper blew back into his jacket pocket. Jack stepped back. He wadded the paper and this time dropped it into the water below, but a breeze gently wafted the paper up and back into his pocket. The paper would not be gone. Jack slipped off the jacket, abandoning it on a bench. The scrap of paper still nestled in the pocket.

He wandered that day down one street to another, making his way across town. His plans for the day were forgotten and when he returned home, the jacket was on the back of the dining room chair, the note still in the right-hand pocket.

That night Jack tossed and turned in his bed, paced the floor, then finally took a match to the note in the fireplace. He watched it burn, ashes falling into the hearth.

When he woke, the note was again in the jacket pocket; even though there were ashes in the fireplace grate. *Didn't I burn it? Why can't I get rid of it?* The radio clicked on and Jimi Hendrix's rendition of the national anthem blared. Jack's fingers played each note on an imaginary guitar. He hadn't played the guitar in nearly fifty years. He was drafted at twenty, served a year and a half in Vietnam, lost his left arm in combat. He looked down awe-struck. He was playing the air guitar with his left arm. It was back. Jack extended the arm, wiggled the fingers. It was his arm. He went to the mirror. As he looked at his reflection, his gray beard disappeared, leaving him pink-cheeked and peach fuzzed. His once-again blond hair hung down to his shoulders. This was his eighteen-year-old self; no longer sixty-seven. *I have another chance.*

Jack inhaled, the tightness in his chest gone, his back straightening as if he was returned to his youth. *I'll do it. I should take this chance before it's too late.*

And as quickly as his left arm was there, it was gone again. Jack looked at his slack sleeve, then his wrinkled face, whiskers and bald head. *For a moment, I was eighteen again.*

What had the man said? Fifty thousand dollars in thirty-six hours? How much time do I have left? That was yesterday. I've only got a few hours left.

He drove his two-year-old Subaru to the lot in Port Angeles and said he needed them to buy it back. He didn't have time to sell it himself. He had paid over thirty thousand. They gave him twenty. He called the number on his American Express credit card and arranged for a cash advance to be deposited. At Key Bank, he transferred money from his savings to fulfill the obligation and ordered the cashier's check, wiping out the balance in his accounts. The teller asked him a lot of questions and acted like he wasn't in his right mind. Jack stayed focused and walked out with the cashier's check in the right pocket of his jacket. His fingers drummed on the paper folded there.

It was raining when Jack caught the next bus heading west toward Forks and disembarked at the junction with Highway 112. He stopped in at *The Dam Bar* and had a burger, fries and several beers. He was excited for the opportunity but worried that it would not come to fruition. *Am I a fool taken in by a carnie?*

The music that night was heavy metal, and the fingers of his right hand tapped to the beat. At one-thirty, he began the three-mile walk to the Elwha Bridge. At the center of the bridge, the rain stopped. He looked around. There was no one in sight. He checked his watch; he was right on time.

What if it was only a dream? What if I'm only an old fool?

He felt an itch in the arm that was no longer there. He reached with his right hand to check for the arm.

"Jump," a voice commanded from the darkness.

"What?" Jack looked around. He saw no one.

"Jump!"

The voice was familiar though. He'd heard it before. *It's the voice of the man in the suit from the carnival tent. The man I'm supposed to meet on the Elwha Bridge with the cashier's check for fifty thousand dollars.*

"Where are you?" Jack said.

The wind rustled through the trees, pushed at Jack's back, shoving him against the waist-high railing.

Jack straddled the railing, then tucked both legs over, and fell into the void. The check wafted in the breeze landing squarely on the bridge at the feet of the man in the dark suit.

* * *

At the busy truck stop, Jack threw his backpack over his shoulder and flicked back his hair, plaited in a single blond braid. A Fender Stratocaster was slung over his other shoulder, his left thumb out. It was turning out to be another hot August day and the temperature was still rising. He was lucky enough to get a ride across Highway 81 toward Syracuse, but he still had a hundred miles to go. *No worries,* he thought, *I've got three days before Woodstock, plenty of time. This is my chance.*

THE FAMOUS FARE

There was something familiar about the man who waited at the curb. He was tall, handsome and smiled as I parked the car. He nodded at me and climbed into the back seat. I started driving for Uber to make a few extra dollars.

"Right on time," he said.

I smiled trying to remember who he was. *Did we know each other? Had I given him a ride recently?*

"Headed to the airport? Which airlines?"

"United," he said.

"International?"

"No," he said.

"Where are you going?" I asked trying to make conversation.

"Home," he said.

Enough, I thought. I'd remember him if he'd ridden with me before. Not much of a talker.

"LA," he said.

"Oh." He surprised me offering that bit of information.

As I threaded through traffic, I kept glancing at him in the rear-view mirror. I couldn't place how I knew him, or why he seemed familiar. He'd catch me looking at him and give me a toothy grin.

Then I knew. It was him. What's his name – that famous movie star. The one in all those hero type movies. His photo is always on the cover of the tabloids in the supermarket.

As those thoughts rushed, I blushed. I must be a sight. My hair's a mess, no makeup. What kind of an impression did I make? I needed to grab a selfie with him.

Driving on the interstate at seventy miles per hour, my right hand rummaged through the contents of my purse pulling out my hairbrush, lipstick, mascara, and cell phone.

I calculated there were several traffic lights between the freeway and the airport terminal and prioritized my actions. First, I took a slightly longer route. At the first stop, I brushed my hair, fluffing it up. At the second stop, I adjusted the rear view mirror and applied mascara. I got a green light at the last intersection, but I can apply lipstick without a mirror.

As I pulled to the curb outside the United terminal, I said, "I'll get your luggage," forgetting that he had none. I jumped out of the car and ran around to the trunk.

He gave me a condescending smile and waited while I asked if I could take a photo with him. I felt the embarrassment redden my cheeks.

Amused at my request, he chuckled, "I'm not who you think I am. Happens all the time."

"But you're another...satisfied customer," I ad-libbed, as I snapped the picture.

THE AUBERGINE SCARF

At the last minute, I tugged the aubergine scarf from its hanger, untangling it from the clutch of two other scarves. *Why do I have so many scarves? Well, for one, I keep knitting them and I am a sucker for a unique one.* In the car, I seat belted, then looped the scarf into a figure eight over my head. *Nice and cozy.* Good thing, since it was already dark and threatening rain. As I maneuvered the car to the major artery into town, I dipped my chin into the folds of the purple scarf, catching a whiff of my perfume.

I wasn't enthusiastic about venturing out tonight but there were people counting on me. I brought the audio equipment and emceed the evening's open mic readings. And I had a story to share. One that I had found humorous, hoping others would too.

It's only a few minutes to town and a bit more to cart everything in and set up. A lot of the regulars show up early and offer to help. It's a great group of people. I warmed up to the idea of being there. I disengaged my scarf from my neck and looped it through the back of a chair, the chair I would sit in. It would be safe there, not fall on the floor or get lost in the shuffle. That is what I thought, then I turned my attention to the readers and guests for the evening.

Wrapping up, I said, "See you all next month," and turned off the microphone. At that point several people started stacking the chairs, others sought one another for conversation. One or two asked me a question or wanted to fill me in on some random gossip. I unplugged the microphone, turned off the amplifier and folded the mic stand. When I turned, my chair had been removed. I carted my belongings out to the hall.

Zoe shouted down the hall to me, "I've got everything; see you at the car."

Everything? I wondered. But a look around didn't turn up anything else. I turned out the lights, picked up my bag and purse, and called back, "Do you have my scarf?"

The elevator door closed but I heard her question, "Scarf?"

* * *

It's reminiscent of a time long ago. My sisters and I took our small children to a county park that offered a train ride. It had been free when we were young, but now they sold tickets. As we headed to the ticket booth, the train rumbled by and at the back of the car was our sister with her three children. One of us yelled out, "Did you get your tickets?" and her reply came in the wind, "Tiiiiiiiiiiickets?" It's a family joke now often bandied about when we were all together.

I thought this as I headed to my car to meet Zoe and collect my audio equipment.

"Sorry about the scarf," she said. "Someone picked it up thinking it was Jennifer's and said she would give it to her."

"It's okay," I said. I'd already arranged to see Jennifer, so figured we would sort out the scarf.

Zoe emailed the following week, "I have tracked down the scarf and will rendezvous to pick it up. What is your address? Will you be home around four?"

I responded with my address but also said that it wasn't urgent.

The next day she advised that her GPS took her on a wild goose chase, and she would check MapQuest when she got home, and try again to return it to me tomorrow.

That night at the local cinema, someone stole her car. She came out of the movie theater and walked to where she left the car. Then she looked around trying to remember where she had parked. (I swear everyone over forty, does this. "I'm sure I left it right here.")

As she relayed this, my mind wandered back to another time. One of the guys I worked with offered to take me to lunch and on the way out of the building, he said, "I'll drive." In the parking lot, he became flustered, then irate. "I left the car here. I always park in this spot." He stomped his foot. We all knew he drove a vintage 1967 dark red Mustang. I looked around the lot as well. Then he shouted, "It's been stolen."

He turned and hightailed it back to the lobby. He yelled for the receptionist to dial 9-1-1. He took the receiver and announced that his car had been stolen. He proceeded to give them the license plate number, the make and model, year, color and finally our address. As he began the litany about how he parked the car that morning at 7:30, he quieted. He took a deep breath. "Sorry, I forgot I dropped it off for an oil change this morning," he said. Then he hung up.

"I'll drive," I said.

This felt a little like that. The police arrived at the cinema and took down all the info about Zoe's car. Meanwhile she called her husband to pick her up. The police waited with her to be sure she was all right.

The next day she called to tell me.

"Too bad about your car," I said.

That's when I remembered another stolen car report from some years back. This car had also been stolen from a cinema parking lot. My friend Suzi was dating Jake. They went to the movies and the parking lot was crowded so they parked further away than they normally did. When the movie let out, the car was nowhere to be found. They searched and searched. Finally, they called the police and reported the car stolen. His insurance asked for additional information. He admitted he fudged the details a bit. In the backseat and trunk of his car he had a broken microwave and four bald tires he was going to dispose of. He reported that he had just purchased four new tires and a new microwave. They provided him with a rental and after some weeks, came through with a generous settlement. He bought a new car and felt good about life.

The theatre complex was huge and the parking lot expansive, additional parking was available in a residential neighborhood.

Six months later Jake received a phone call from the local police that they located his car. They wanted him to identify it. He wondered about the condition now that he had replaced it.

The car was found parked at the end of a dead-end

road behind the theatres. From the dirt on it, it appeared to have been there the entire six months it had been missing. The insurance company sent a representative to take a look. He reported that the only damage was that the four new tires in the trunk had been replaced with bald ones and the new microwave was old and broken. No one said Jake lied about the car missing, but he had to reimburse the insurance company the full benefit. Now he owned two cars.

* * *

Only Zoe's car really was stolen. It was not in the parking lot or nearby. "Anything of value in the car?" the insurance company asked.

"Only my friend's scarf," she said.

A couple of weeks went by and I forgot about the scarf. I hoped that someday I might run into someone wearing it. I could accost them about its origin. Zoe was still apologizing every time I saw her. I kept telling her it wasn't worth that much. In fact, I could not recall where I got it or how much I paid for it. As more time passed, I could only say it was purple and knit – no, not wool, and it was long and there was some sort of ruffle. I wondered if it still smelled of Opium.

Over time the exact shape and color of the scarf morphed in my memory. I bought a new dress with an aubergine accent and I thought how that scarf would have perfectly complemented the dress. I started shopping online for a new perfect scarf.

Zoe called. They found her car. Apparently some kids took it for a joyride. When it ran out of gas, they left it on the side of the road and the police had it towed into their storage yard. She came back after ID-ing it. "I've got your scarf," she chortled.

We met for coffee the next day where she ceremoniously handed me the scarf, I scowled. *Was this my scarf?* The color was wrong. It wasn't quite as nice as I remembered. I thanked her, but I could see that she was saddened by my lack of enthusiasm. I put it on trying to rally. I was thinking this wasn't the same scarf. She went out and bought it or the thugs left this one in its place, but as I sniffed it, there was the faint scent of Opium. It was indeed my scarf.

As A Fox

"She's as crazy as a fox," Sam said.

That's what he said when she sold him her Audi sport coupe and turned the proceeds into a down payment on a condo. But because they were dating, she still drove the Audi.

"She's just plain looney," he said when she left him standing at the altar and took off on the honeymoon without him. "I'll show her," he said.

We waited and watched. What was he going to do? It wasn't long before his plan was unveiled. Brittany fancied herself a dog breeder and took deposits on future litters from her pedigreed Cocker Spaniel, Sadie. When the bitch came into heat, Sam stole onto the property with his dog. Sparky was a yellow Lab and Poodle mix.

Soon after, Brittany rubbed her hands together and took more reservations. For a dog like Sadie a litter of four or five was normal, but the vet told her she was carrying eight, maybe ten. Brittany was delighted. She didn't pay much attention to the vet who warned her that this might be too much for a six-year-old dog. He suggested they terminate the pregnancy and try again later. She would hear nothing of it.

Of course, the prepaid reservations were for pedigreed Cocker Spaniels. Buyers were willing to shell out two thousand dollars each. "A lot of money for a dog," Sam said, then he whistled. But he said that when they were in love and planning a future together. None of that money came his way. Now he chuckled when anyone talked about Brittany and her puppy fortune.

The vet shook his head when he saw Sadie next, her belly hung low to the ground and there was a definite waddle in her gait. He examined her hips and spine and clucked his tongue that this was too much for her frame.

Brittany asked, "A re there still ten puppies?" Together they peered at the screen and watched as the sonogram showed their puppy bodies paddling about in the amniotic fluid. "Eight, nine...ten!" Brittany counted, and clapped her hands together.

"She's carrying a lot of weight," the vet said, knowing that Brittany would not pay attention. There are dog lovers and then there are dog lovers, he thought. Sometimes he daydreamed about taking dogs away from people that did not put their animals first. He patted Sadie affectionately. "Not much longer to go, girl. Are you sure the sire is a Cocker Spaniel?" he asked.

"Of course," Brittany said. "She's a pure bred. I would never cross breed my dog."

"It's unusual for a Cocker to have such a large litter," he said. "And the puppies seem larger than her last litter."

"Oh, they'll be fine!" she said. "Come, Sadie, let's go home."

When the puppies came, everyone said they were adorable, then quickly asked. "What kind are they?"

Brittany knew she had a problem. The vet took DNA samples. There was no connection to the sire Brittany had paid for stud service. These were not pure-bred Cocker Spaniel puppies. "Well, what are they?" she asked Dr. Winters, tapping her foot impatiently.

"If I had to give them a name...I'd say they are a mix of Cocker Spaniel and...Golden Retriever. There's some Poodle in them, too. But they are the cutest puppies I've ever seen. You shouldn't have any problem finding them homes." He watched her reaction to the news.

"I've been robbed," Brittany cried.

The vet shrugged his shoulders, cradling one of the puppies. "Do you know anyone with a Golden Doodle?"

An image of Sam and his half breed, Sparky, flashed in her mind. "Oh, shih-tzu," she said.

Sam waited for the irate phone call, the accusation. He was prepared for her anger. The call never came. Instead Brittany advertised the dogs as mini-doodles and raised the price to three thousand dollars and sold off the entire litter in no time. He saw her ad online, she referred to them as "Cockerdoodles."

"Well, I'll be," Sam said, "she is as sly as a fox."

THE BANANA BLUNDER

"That's a twenty-three-thousand-dollar mistake," the manager of Neighborly Market sneered at the junior buyer.

Sylvie nodded. "I...I understand," she stuttered. Lowering her head, the memories flooded back. She placed orders on Tuesday with Consolidated Produce. On the previous Tuesday she came in late because of her court appearance, requesting a divorce and sole custody of her two young children. Her ex stood there in his jail garb scowling and spewing untruths about her. Their attorneys argued. Really argued there in court with the judge pounding his gavel and the bailiff shouting, "Order in the court, order in the court."

It was a wonder Sylvie made it into work that day. Then she blundered.

Sylvie wondered what Mr. MacDonald would be screaming if she had omitted a zero instead of inserting an extra one. Instead of placing the weekly order for one thousand pounds of bananas, she ordered ten thousand pounds.

"How the hell are we going to move an extra nine thousand pounds of bananas?" Mr. MacDonald groaned.

"Let me work on it. I'll do my best...and if I don't, I guess I'm gonna owe you the difference."

Sylvie's cousin Frank worked on the receiving dock. He had raised the alarm about the abundance of bananas.

"I flubbed big time," she said.

"Let's get the word out and see if we can't sell them off."

Sylvie nodded. "I'll call the family."

Neighborly Market was the grocery store for the little town of Skokes and the outlying area. Sylvie's family was well-established there; her mother taught at the high school, her sister worked at the local newspaper and her dad ran the radio station.

Sylvie called her mother first.

"Hold on Sylvie, if you price the bananas so that you pay for them and make the same profit you would have on a thousand pounds, you'll be out of hot water."

Sylvie told her what they cost, and what they usually charged.

"Price 'em low," her mother said, "and call your father."

Her father stifled a chuckle, then set up an on-air interview with Mr. MacDonald.

Sylvie put up signs in the store: "Bananas on sale at twenty-nine cents a pound." Sylvie also texted and tweeted, and posted it on Facebook.

The editor of the local newspaper agreed to print something on the front page about the big banana bonanza when Sylvie's sister asked. The paper hit the newsstands two days later.

On the third day after the delivery of the ten thousand pounds of bananas, they had already moved a third of them. Local restaurants bought them up and the bakery, too. There was going to be a surplus of banana bread sometime soon.

You'd think that mentioning her name would feel like a slap in her face, but it had the opposite effect. Everyone who knew Sylvie, and that was everyone in Skokes, showed up to support her.

By Friday night they had to post a sign, "Bananas Sold Out."

The following Tuesday, Sylvie ordered one thousand pounds of bananas, then carefully checked and double-checked her figures. Proudly she never made another mistake like that.

You wouldn't think that was true if you shopped at the Neighborly Market because every month since they have a "Sylvie Oops Sale." As it turned out, they not only sold all those bananas but no one who came in for bananas, left with only the bananas. Sylvie directed they put the bananas next to their highest grossing products. The store broke records in numbers of transactions, sales, and profits from the banana blunder.

Subsequently, Sylvie was promoted to senior buyer, and marketing consultant all because of that one zero.

NOISES

Taped to my front door was a note scrawled on binder paper, "We have to talk about the barking."

I read the note, ripped it from the door and fumed into the house. Another note from the same neighbor.

Last time I went across the street and tried to explain about the dog's barking.

He wasn't buying any of it. "Either you do something about it, or I will."

I took to walking the dog two, then three times a day, making a big deal of passing by the neighbor's house so he could see that I was doing something about it.

His complaints about my dog's barking were not limited to my dog or his barking. I heard the Labs down the street barking, but he called my number. "Do something," he said then, he hung up.

"But it's not my dog..." I said to the dial tone.

Eventually, I realized there was no reasoning with him. Any noise disturbance became my dog's barking. The roofers two blocks away began hammering at seven on Saturday and I got the terse phone call at 7:15, then again at 8:05. He wouldn't listen to what I had to say, only voiced his complaint, then he'd disconnect.

I took my cell phone around the neighborhood capturing the roofers, the gardener with the loud blower, the lawnmowers, the chain saw, the other dogs barking and created a video surveillance account of all the noises in the neighborhood with date and time stamps. I left the DVD on his doorstep.

For two days, I thought the whining had stopped. I didn't want to do a victory dance yet, but I was feeling confident. The next morning the geese flew overhead beginning their migration. "Honk honk honk." From after six to just before nine, "Honk honk honk."

"Shut the dog up," he screamed from the phone.

"It's the geese," I said but I swallowed the 'you idiot.'"

I watched his house, his comings and goings. When I saw him pull out of his driveway, I sighed with relief.

My husband suggested it was time to move. "It's getting too crowded, too civilized around here," he said.

"But it's the principle of the matter," I argued. "Most of the time when he complains it is not even our dog."

His glare told me right or wrong, it was beside the point. We needed to move away for our privacy.

I tidied the yard and fumed about the mess of things. I liked my house, had put a lot of labor into my flower beds. The dog lay in the grass nearby watching me. Two dogs ran in the street without leashes, three other dogs barked from behind their fences. Two Harley Davidson motorcycles cruised the neighborhood, their mufflers barely quieting the engines' roar.

When Mr. Mackay pulled the rip cord on his diesel-powered chipper feeding in the limbs from his pruning, I covered my ears and headed back inside, "All that noise and he only complains about your barking," I said to my dog,

My husband met with real estate agents about putting the house on the market.

It was then the complainer pulled into his driveway. I ran across the street. "Why do you keep calling me? I know my dog barks some of the time, but often you call when it is some other noise." I stood hands on my hips demanding a response.

He looked at me. "Oh, you're the lady in charge of noise complaints. Right?"

"No! I am your neighbor," and I pointed to my house across the street.

He bent down and patted my dog. "Nice dog."

"What are you saying? You thought I was the one to complain to?"

"Yes, I thought I understood..."

I laughed. "Please don't call me anymore."

I fairly danced across the street as the estate agent was putting the For Sale sign in our front yard.

I went in search of my husband. "It's all a mistake. He thought I was the complaint department for the neighborhood."

"You don't want to move do you?" my husband asked.

"No, I don't. I like it here," I said.

"Okay," I'll call the agent tomorrow.

* * *

The truth is that our dog is a decoy, one to stop the rise of rumors. For when the full moon rises, my husband prowls into the yard and howls at the moon.

DRIFTED AWAY

Online dating was as bad as Russian roulette. It began with a flurry of emails that led to a phone call. Putting a voice to the words made all the difference in the world. We tentatively revealed facts about ourselves and were delighted to find so many common threads. That first phone call lasted five hours, till three in the morning. Reluctantly but insistently, we said good night because we both had to go to work in a few hours. He said he would call me the following evening at nine.

That afternoon clouds gathered, and rain fell. It overran the gutters gushing into the streets. My drive home in the dark was treacherous. The news reported creeks and rivers overrunning their banks, electrical power lines downed, and still more rain forecast. Clouds blotted out the moon making it harder to see the road ahead. I navigated the roadway for an hour. Traffic was light, and I kept my high beams on as much as possible. There was a bridge between me and home, one where the river often overflowed its banks making the road impassable. I listened for news about that section of road. There was no mention of it. If all was well, I'd be in home by nine, in time for his call.

My heart soared at the prospect of a romance. The stars seemed aligned for us, with so much in common.

He had such a nice voice.

As I turned onto the road that crossed the river, I could see flashing lights ahead. I slowed. *Was the bridge out? Was the road closed?*

Closer I could see that the flashing lights were cautionary, warning of water on the roadway. There was no closure. I breathed a sigh of relief, and downshifted into low, crossing the bridge through several inches of water. My headlights flashed on something in the road ahead. A downed tree made the road impassable. I didn't have a chainsaw or anything with which to move it. I had no choice. I pulled out my cell phone and called emergency service to report the tree down. I left my vehicle with its flashers on to alert other drivers.

It was a quarter to nine. My house was only a half-mile up the road, and I could cover that distance easily. I buttoned my raincoat and rummaged around in the back of the car for an umbrella. I always kept an umbrella in my car. I usually kept a pair of boots for walking around in the mud as well, but I had cleaned the car two days before and had not reloaded my emergency gear. No boots. No umbrella. I looked down at my feet. The new Nike trainers. *How much had I paid for them? Was it worth it?*

I closed the car door and clambered over the tree. Then with water running over the tops of my shoes, I started the climb up the hill. Silt from the river had been pushed up another six feet and I slogged through the mud. The rain continued and I hadn't gone far before feeling soaked through, cold to the bone. I got off the road and walked under the tall firs trying to get relief from the rain. I passed several homes and the lights within gave me hope that the power and phone lines were still in service.

The clock chimed nine as I stopped at the door and took off my wet shoes and clothing. In my damp underwear, I ran through the house to wrap myself in a blanked. I wanted to take a hot shower but afraid I'd miss his call. I put the kettle on for tea. When it whistled, I ran to answer the phone, only to realize it was the tea kettle.

At half past, I decided he wasn't going to call after all. It was such a letdown. Maybe his power was out, maybe the phone lines were down. It was then I realized I didn't know his number. He had called me. I sent him an email. No matter what I told myself, nothing would relieve the disappointment. I went into the bathroom and turned on the shower, time to get warmed up. The hot water streamed over me. The lights blinked and went out. Despite the darkness, I emptied the hot water tank luxuriating in the warmth.

The next morning, I put on my rain gear and boots and trekked down to my car. The tree had not been removed and as I climbed over it, I saw that my car was nowhere to be seen. The river no longer flowed over the bridge, but half the road had been washed away, the half where I left my car. Thinking I had been a fool to leave my car because of a phone call, I called the insurance company.

He never called or answered my emails. I went over that long conversation, the interest seemed mutual. The promise of a romance drifted away like my car.

BICYCLE DREAMS

Three nights in a row I wake from terrible nightmares. Dreams of bicyclists meeting their death. The scenarios are different, the players the same. I wander the halls trying to erase the terror.

But the terror exists in wakefulness as well.

* * *

My daughter sat with me; we laughed and drank wine. It was a first for us, a time without judgement or blame. A time of two women accepting each other, at peace with our shared history. All past hurts were set aside proving that tough love does work. Near midnight she kissed me on the cheek, climbed onto her bicycle and wheeled off into the night. She lived a short distance away.

As I cleared the glasses to the kitchen, I saw her purse sitting on the floor. She would need it. I couldn't fathom how she had forgotten it. If I hurried, I could catch her.

I backed the car out of the garage and negotiated the winding dark road watching for her. At the bottom of the hill, I turned right knowing that I should meet her along this road before she crossed into the downtown streets. There was no sign of her, and I wondered if she had taken another route, or had I passed her without realizing it? I slowed, contemplating these options.

Then I hit something. There was a thump and a screech of metal. I stopped the car and jumped out.

In the road was a bicycle wheel, mangled. *What is it doing here? Is it hers?*

I called out her name. "Gloria?"

The night breeze blew it back in my face.

My headlights shone on the open roadway ahead. I went to the car for the flashlight. The beam was unsteady and weak.

"Gloria?" I called again.

I got into the car, slowly turning it around, and flashed the high beams onto the road I had travelled. It was empty. I got out of the car and walked along the roadway.

"Gloria?"

Further back the way I had come, there was a glint of metal on the far side of the road. I jogged to the site. There lay a bicycle; its front wheel missing.

"Gloria?" I whispered.

I stepped into the tall grass and saw a body. I prayed that it was not her, that it was someone else. *"Oh God, please not my girl."*

I knelt beside the body of a woman. She wore the same cut off blue jeans, the red sweatshirt and black tennis shoes that Gloria had worn this evening.

"Gloria," I said, "please God let her be alright." I ran back to the car, taking her cell phone from her purse. I turned it on and dialed 9-1-1.

"What is the nature of your emergency?"

"Help," I said. "My daughter's been hit."

"Where are you?"

"At the end of Hill drive, just where it crosses Jackson," I said.

"Is she conscious?"

"No."

"Is she breathing?"

"I don't know."

"Are you with her?"

"I came back to the car for the phone."

"An ambulance is on its way. Go back to her. Stay on the phone. What happened?"

"Someone hit her. She was on her bicycle…"

My mind replayed what I had said. "Someone…" *Was it me? Did I hit my own daughter as she rode? Was that sound I heard me hitting her bicycle? I ran over the wheel; I admit to that. But what happened first?*

"Does she have a pulse?"

"I think so, it's weak." My hand moved from her limp wrist to her throat. She was laying on her side, tossed like a rag doll. "Should I move her?"

"No. Help is on its way. What is her name?"

"Gloria, her name is Gloria." *Why didn't I see her? She had reflectors on her bicycle, on her helmet. She had a headlight. I didn't see that light?*

"What is your name?"

"Huh? Oh, Donna, Donna Adams." *They will ask me if I was drinking. How much did I drink? How much did she drink? We finished a bottle of wine…over the evening. What time did we start? What time is it now?*

"Are you hurt?"

I heard the siren at that point. I gulped fresh air trying to sober myself. "Please God," I prayed again. What I wanted was to erase the last fifteen minutes. Why didn't I see her purse and call out to her before she got on the bike? Before she came down the hill. Before...

* * *

The following night, I dreamed we had another cataclysmic argument over her lack of ambition and poor choice in men. I raised my voice, she screamed and ran out of the house. Only for some reason, we were in the mountains. When she got onto the bicycle, she rode along a rocky ridge only inches from the steep side of a canyon. I yelled at her again, and she turned to look back at me.

Did she raise her arm to wave me off or was she going to use it to send me an obscene gesture? With her right hand off the handlebars and her head turned over her right shoulder, the front wheel veered left and off the narrow path. I watched the bicycle carry Gloria over the edge as they both fell into the canyon. I heard the bike crash and bang against rocks, metal clinking as it fell apart.

* * *

In tonight's dream, I ran over her while driving in a rainstorm. I couldn't see the road in front of me. Then there was the sound of metal crunching under my tires and a thump that could only be a body. It was enough to wake me, enough to keep the car in the garage another day, enough to make me roam the house in the wee hours of the morning waiting for dawn.

I dialed her number, but she didn't answer. If only

she would answer. If only I could accept these dreams as nightmares.

If only there was no mangled bicycle in the trunk of my car.

BOOMERANG

It wasn't because of a geography lesson but the distribution of a toy that I became aware of Australia. The boomerang was an obtusely angled slice of wood which when thrown would spin back to the thrower. Totally dependable. Repeatable. It was awesome. It was distributed by Wham-O, the same people who brought us the Hula Hoop and the Frisbee. Advertised on television, I gazed in awe at its return to the thrower, over and over again. Did this really work? What were its magical powers? Could anyone learn to do it?

That Christmas my sister, Kellie, unwrapped a brightly wrapped box that held a Boomerang. It was the best present under the tree, though several were more expensive. Outside my father scanned the instructions, then hurled the toy into the air. It flew across the driveway and far into the ten-acre orchard which was our "backyard." We watched in amazement. It turned and came back but fell short of returning to Dad's hand. Over and over again, he practiced as we children stood begging at his feet. "Let me, let me." "It's mine, I got it from Santa." "I can do it, I know I can."

He had to take a step forward, hand outstretched, before it came to him. That's when he handed it to Kellie.

She stepped up like she was going to bat, and with all her nine-year-old might, threw it as she had seen Dad demonstrate.

I should add that my dad is right-handed as are all of us. Kellie is the lone lefty in our family. Her toss did not follow the same trajectory. If Dad's went left, her's went right and instead of turning and coming back, her's fell from the air and landed in the dirt. Far down the path through the orchard.

We raced out to retrieve it.

Dad yelled, "just throw it back towards me."

Kellie looked at the toy, turning it over to see if there was a "this side up" instruction. Then she shrugged her shoulders and hurled it toward Dad. We waited watching for the boomerang to turn and come back. Again, it went in a straight path, right into Dad's shins. He was hopping mad and retreated into the house.

"Let me try," I whined. She glowered at me but handed it over. I stood like Dad and tried in every way to repeat what I had seen him do. I tossed the boomerang and as I prayed for it to make the return flight, it did. Kellie stomped her feet and tore it out of my hands. She dashed it to the ground and kicked it.

The two younger sisters picked it up and threw it about, not with the same care and precision. When Patty tried, the damn thing came right back to her. Kellie had enough and grabbed it.

"It's mine," she said. With boomerang in hand, she tromped off into the middle of the orchard. "Leave me alone," she shouted back should anyone consider following her.

At dinner, Dad asked Kellie if she had any luck in getting the boomerang to return.

She looked down, moving the food around on her plate and said she lost it.

After breakfast the next morning, we formed a search party, weaving our way through the trees, eyes downcast, but sometimes looking upward into the branches. We did not find the boomerang.

In the Spring, the orchardist was busy. He needed to cultivate the ground and get ready for irrigation. In turning the soil, he spied the boomerang.

"Kellie, Kellie," he yelled as he jumped off the tractor in our driveway.

We ran out to see why he was calling. Once he brought us a jack rabbit which we tried to tame. We put it in a doghouse with chicken wire over the doorway. We fed it carrots and lettuce and gave it clean water. But one day it chewed its way through the chicken wire, never again to be seen. We decided it was alright as each of us girls had deep red gashes down our chest from its back legs clawing as we held it close.

"Kellie, I found it," he said. In his hands, he clutched the boomerang.

Kellie took it and scuffed her way around the back of the barn. Bad mood was written all over her, so we kept clear.

At dinner, Patty announced that John had found Kellie's boomerang. Dad said, "Kellie, we'll go have another practice after dinner."

Kellie glowered, "I threw it and it went up on the barn roof."

Now there was a place none of us went.

But in the Summer, the cherry plum tree was full of fruit, small cherry-sized plums. When Grandmother visited, she made jam from the fruit.

"Girls climb up on that roof and get me some bucketfuls," she instructed.

It was easy to climb up on the abandoned chicken coop next to the barn. I put the ladder in place and went up, Patty and Debby followed. Each with a bucket which we filled with only the best of the fruit. If it was squishy or the birds had got to it first, we left it or kicked it to the ground. With three full buckets, Granny would have plenty. I climbed down with one bucket then did it two more times. The younger girls were good pickers, but too small to handle the bucket and the ladder.

On seeing me come in, mom asked, "Did you clean off the roof?"

I shook my head.

"Take the broom and sweep it, no reason to leave all that up there to rot."

I dragged the broom and climbed the ladder one more time. I swept the roof, pushing the leaves, fruit and other debris to the ground. Where the tree branches tangled in the roof of the barn, I saw the boomerang. That was the upside for having to pick the cherries and clean the roof. I couldn't wait to show Kellie.

She took one look at it and dissolved into tears. I followed her as she raced up the stairs to the bedroom we shared.

"I hate that stupid thing," she cried.

"I'll help you," I said.

"No, I hate it. I buried it in the orchard…"

"And John found it."

"I threw it up on the roof where no one could find it…"

"And I found it," I said.

She glared at me.

"I guess you can see that it does work. It keeps coming back to you."

THE COWBOY

Bobby Silverado never knew his dad. Instead he watched a steady stream of men befriend his mother. She called them her cowboys. They wore boots, hats, and most had big silver belt buckles. Bobby kept track of all this and longed to be a cowboy.

On his eighth birthday someone gave him a second-hand Stetson which was too big, but that never stopped Bobby from wearing it. A pair of cowboy boots were found forgotten under his mama's bed, and he claimed them. By stuffing socks in the toes of the boots, he could clomp around in them, feeling much like the cowboy he wanted to be. Bobby watched westerns on television and imagined himself riding a horse when he straddled the back of the couch. That's what he was doing, whooping it up like he was riding with the gang, when he leaned too far, and fell out the window. Landing on the awning over the grocery store three flights below, he rolled to the edge and dropped straight down into the cardboard box of watermelon. It was just enough for the sides of the box to split, and the watermelons rolled across the sidewalk into the street. Traffic snarled, horns honked, and it was some time before anyone noticed the boy with only one boot on. His other leg was bent at an odd angle.

The nearby fire department responded to the call and the paramedics assessed the damage. Bobby Silverado spent three days in the hospital where his broken leg was pinned back together, and a cast plastered on. His mother was cautioned to keep him indoors and quiet while it healed. She didn't know how to explain that he was indoors when it happened, and she had told him to keep quiet while she rested.

The window was repaired, and the couch moved across the room against the solid wall. Bobby decided he had enough of the cowboy life and turned to thoughts of being a fireman.

DEAD AIR

Ron became fascinated with radio at an early age. His Grandfather pulled him onto his lap and together they listened to serials. Neither of them lost that interest when television came along. In high school, Ron devised his own broadcast and played tunes in the early evening after school. As a sophomore he won a ribbon at the local science fair for his demonstration showing how AM and FM radio waves worked.

As much as he loved radio, he loved his rock and roll. He would often DJ for school dances. He had no interest in attending college until his counselor pointed out that some schools had their own radio station. With that knowledge, he applied to Cal Poly in San Luis Obispo and started his radio career.

While a student, he had his own program and helped out learning the ins and outs of a radio station. In his senior year, he was able to pull a late-night shift on a small local station. He read the news and weather and recorded the station identification. After graduation he got a weekend shift and recorded community service announcements.

An opportunity arose for him to host a nightly show at a weekly salary of three hundred dollars, but it was a highbrow classical station. Not Ron's type of music. He stayed but spent weekends at rock and roll venues looking for another opportunity.

Things always happen in mysterious ways. It was at one of these venues where there was a battle of the bands, the emcee lost his voice. Ron was working backstage setting up equipment, and was asked to step in. He knew he wasn't anyone's first choice, but he vowed to wow them so that by the end of the weekend, they would be wanting him to come back. He had a quick wit and could ad lib. When he shot out a barb and got a laugh from the audience, he was on fire. He never let up on the banter and got a round of applause at the end of the evening.

That was enough to pique the interest of the events coordinator and another DJ. Suddenly he was in demand. They wanted him to host another music event and a local radio station called to see if he would consider an afternoon program. He knew the station well; it was in the top five where he wanted to work. He jumped at the job.

He took any emcee spots that came up as long as they didn't interfere with his radio career. It was a good thing because he was in demand and those who enjoyed his presence on the stage, followed him into radio. And it worked the other way, as well. Soon the radio station was talking about creating their own battle of the bands and, of course, wanted Ron to host them. What he wanted now was to move from the afternoon programing to drive time. He knew they wouldn't move him there right away, but his second choice was weeknights, and he got that. Now he was working six days a week for the radio station and making good money. He was living the life he always dreamed.

At his ten-year college reunion his fame was known, and one of his old instructors asked him to speak to the current broadcasting class. Ron was delighted. He planned his speech wanting to impart the importance of never leaving dead air. More important, was how to fill the space without resorting to inane conversation. He recommended that they take improv classes over in the drama department and know their subject. He knew the history of rock and roll, who wrote the songs, who the original artists were, who impacted whom and lusted to do live interviews with his idols on the air. Everything Ron did was magic. He was a rock star in his own right.

Ron eventually was offered a more lucrative job in another market. That meant uprooting his family and moving across the country. The upside was his dream job; a very successful rock station in a huge market that was able to attract the rock and roll legends. He would get to spin records, give his insight on the industry and interview guest performers. There was talk of a possible jump to television.

During a shift something happened, and the record player wouldn't play. The technician was called, and he fiddled with this and that. Ron sat watching him through the window and told the audience about silly moments during the battle of the bands years when the now famous bands were unknown. He talked about the greats he had seen play before anyone remembered their names, Janis Joplin, Carlos Santana, Jimi Hendrix. The phone lines lit up and he decided to take the calls on the air, the callers wanted to know more. He took several calls and more kept coming in. It was always good for a disc jockey to know that someone was listening. The technician signaled that he had everything working again. Management patted him on the back. "Good thing we've got you when the equipment goes haywire. There is no dead air when you are on."

Twenty years passed and the music scene changed. Radio was changing. Things were becoming more and more automated. Many stations didn't even have live announcers, they just ran an automated feed – the same thing playing across the country. Ron felt lucky to be well-established and working for the most popular rock and roll station. Then things changed. The station was sold, and the new buyer wanted to go a different way. He thought Ron was a dinosaur and replaced him with a young disc jockey who was one of the first to be called a shock-jock. Rather than educate the listeners about rock and roll, he pulled pranks on listeners and with a side kick ran a banter of insanity between songs. The music became second place to their shenanigans. "That's what listeners want on their commute to work each day," the station manager told Ron. Ron was moved to the evening hours once again. "A step backward," he said to himself. He felt confident that his loyal fans would follow him to the new time, but they turned out to be fickle. In the evenings they watched their laugh-track filled sitcoms.

Ron tried to bring back his call-in show, but only one or two calls came in, and one of them was his producer. This was a sad way to end his long standing and lucrative radio career. His wife suggested he retire, call it quits, move to Florida. He couldn't envision doing anything other than radio. What else was there for him? There had always been radio.

It was on a Tuesday evening in the last hour of his program when Ron succumbed and nearly twenty minutes of dead air was broadcast from the booth before anyone took notice.

DESTINATION

Marjorie and William Sterling boarded the cruise ship via wheelchairs. While both could walk, this saved a lot of time and stress, and alleviated falls. They were taken immediately to their stateroom, one with a wide balcony overlooking the San Francisco Bay. William breathed a sigh and said, "This is the way to go. First class."

"Indeed," Marjorie said, unpacking a small carry-on.

"The view is splendid, better than I would have thought."

The steward hovered. "Is there anything I can bring you now? We'll leave the harbor in two hours. Dinner will be served at seven. Would you like to dine in your room tonight?"

"Is that offered?" Marjorie asked.

"Of course. We make every effort on these senior cruises to make your journey as pleasant as possible. You can fill out the menu on the in-room computer."

Marjorie looked at William and he nodded, "Yes, we'll dine in tonight. Thank you."

The steward bowed and opened the door to exit. Then he turned, "I almost forgot, there is celebratory champagne in your refrigerator. Would you like me to open and pour for you before I leave?"

"Oh, that would be fabulous," Marjorie said.

He deftly uncorked the bottle and poured two flutes, then set the bottle in the ice bucket before leaving the room.

Marjorie made her way to the veranda and sat down. "This is the life."

"It is my dear," William said taking the seat beside her.

"Here's to fifty-three years together." They clinked their glasses and sipped the champagne.

"And to what lies beyond," William said.

"Enjoyed all of it because of you," Marjorie said, patting William's hand.

"Everything settled then?"

"It is. Customer Relations will mail the letter to Holly."

* * *

On Friday, Holly received a letter from her parents. She turned the envelope over in her hand. It was unusual for her mother to write, she usually called. Holly wondered when she last spoke with her parents. Her life was busy with work and family. She felt guilty because her parents were alone across the country and her father's health was waning.

She tucked the envelope into her pocket, planning to read it during her son's soccer game later. Only rain cancelled the game, and she picked up pizza for the family that night.

Saturday her cell phone rang.

"Yes?" She said into the phone.

"Is this Holly Warburton?"

"It is," she said warily, assuming the caller was a solicitor, ready to disconnect to avoid hearing an offer.

"This is Micah McLaren and I am calling regarding Marjorie and William Sterling."

"Yes?" Holly said.

"Sorry to call with bad news…"

"Bad news? What bad news? Who is this?"

"Micah McLaren with the Valkyrie Cruise Line…"

"My parents? What cruise?" She stopped where she stood in the grocery store. "What? You must be wrong. My parents are at home…"

"Did you receive a letter from them yesterday?"

"I did…" *But I never opened it. Is it still in my jacket pocket? How would this person know that they sent me a letter? Is this a scam?*

"I am sure this is a shock, but I need to advise you that while at sea, Marjorie and William Sterling peacefully went in their sleep. As this occurred in international waters and per their request, their bodies were buried at sea…"

"What?" Holly plopped down in the cereal aisle. The colorful boxes lining the shelves faded into the background. "They're dead?" she said focusing on Tony the Tiger.

"Yes, sorry to have to advise you this way, but this is as they requested."

"What do you mean as they requested? Surely they did not know they would die in their sleep. What are you saying?" People stopped in the aisle, offering assistance. Holly waved them off.

His voice changed. He spoke deliberately as if he was accustomed to speaking with hysterical women.

"Then you have not read their letter? You did not know that they were taking this cruise?"

"No. What cruise are you talking about?"

"It is the Valkyrie Cruise Line, we offer premium senior cruises…"

"My father is terminally ill. I can't see why they were taking a cruise at this time. My mother was in perfect health." Holly sobbed. *Could this be true?* She found herself asking Snap Crackle and Pop. The man on the oatmeal box gazed back kindly.

"You need to read the letter."

"Okay, okay. I have to go home to get it. I'm at the grocery store…"

"Go home. Read the letter. Call me if you need more information."

Holly rushed out of the grocery store, leaving her half-full cart in the cereal aisle. Her phone still in her hand, she dialed her mother's number. It rang and rang, then a message that the number was no longer in use. *What the hell?* She dialed their landline. Again, it rang and rang and then the message, "This number has been disconnected."

At home she stormed into the house and searched through the coats hanging in the hall closet. *Which one did I wear yesterday? What can the letter say that will explain this?*

Her husband, Roger, called to the kids, "Let's help mom with the groceries." They were out the door before Holly realized what they were doing and then back as quickly.

"Honey? Where are the groceries? I thought you went shopping?" Roger asked.

"Uh huh, I did, but ... Here it is." Holly pulled the envelope from the pocket.

"What, what happened?"

"Oh, the damn letter." The envelope, a number ten, like a business mailing, but it was in her mother's handwriting. Holly tore it open and sunk down on the arm of a chair.

"What's that?" Roger asked with concern.

Holly waved her hand at her husband. She read, then her breath caught, and she let out a sob.

"What is it?" He moved across the room to read over her shoulder. "Who's taking a cruise? Who is this from?"

"It's from my mom. She and dad went on a cruise..."

"I thought he was in hospice..."

"He was..." Holly dissolved into her husband's embrace, sobbing. "They're dead."

"What? Who's dead? Your father?"

"My parents. They died at sea ..."

He let go a long string of questions, but Holly was unable to answer. The kids stood in the doorway watching their parents, afraid to ask any questions. Finally, Roger took the hand-written letter from Holly and read it through.

Dear Holly,

Your father is dying, and the pain is intolerable. The doctors said there is nothing more they can do, but to try and keep him comfortable. I could not stand by and watch, and there is nothing more I could do to ease his journey. We have watched many of our friends suffer. It's horrible for the dying partner, often worse for the one left behind.

When we learned about this cruise, it seemed the perfect solution. We will exit together and in a beautiful surrounding. We'll leave no funeral expense or arrangements to burden you. Our will leaves all our assets to you, and we are proud to say that we leave no debts. You have been the daughter we always wanted, and we will miss you but hope that we may reunite with you in the hereafter (if there is one).

With love,
Mother and Father

Roger bent and picked up the envelope from the floor. Inside was a glossy color brochure, a cruise ship on the cover advertising "Your Final Destination" offered by the Valkyrie Cruise Line. It touted that patrons could embark at any port of call and select their departure date within the one-week sailing time. During their stay on board, they would have access to all the luxuries and services. A list of options under "Remains" allowed the passengers to choose between having their bodies returned to shore or buried at sea. A shaky hand had circled the latter. And under "Accommodations," there was another circle for the veranda suite. Roger cursed when he read the next section. Under "Demise," the choices included "Dinner and a Movie," "Injection," and "Drug of Choice." He hurriedly closed the brochure before Holly could read the circled selection.

Holly and her husband visited the local travel agency and learned that this final destination cruise is one of many services offered to seniors. Ships leave filled to capacity every Saturday and return empty the following Saturday. "And that is just here in our port," the woman behind the desk said. "They have many ports of call."

Information on the service was readily available. Hospice caretakers knew about it and suggested it to their patients. For some there was free passage when they could not afford it. "Not as many of the luxuries nor the veranda suite for those," one man said, "but it is a better way to go than expiring in a lonely hospital ward and being buried without a grave marker. Isn't it?"

At last Holly went to check their home. It was apparent they had no plans of returning. On the kitchen table was an official-looking envelope marked "Final Instructions." Inside were details about bank accounts, insurance policies and the deed to the house. Closets and cupboards had been cleared out. The refrigerator stood empty. Marjorie left some things – perhaps more to make Holly feel that she was gone for good. These things had been dear to Marjorie, pictures of family and close friends, her favorite books.

At the memorial service Holly said, "My parents chose to obey their marriage vow till death do us part, and even in death they went together."

THE DETECTIVE

This was not the first time Davo Fost encountered disappointment, nor would it be the last. He pushed back from his desk and sighed. It never seemed to matter what assistance he provided, people could not be counted on to make progress, or to correct the errors of their ways. He stood and walked across the room. They scoffed at his research, and no longer needed him. He'd been warned that guards were coming to remove him. He shook his head. They did not know what they needed nor how to get it.

Davo worked at maintaining a familiar appearance. He was a tall man, nearly seven feet tall, taller than most of the men in this population. His hair was gray around the temples, and he wore a full beard which was the current fashion. He paused one last time and looked around the room. This had been his office and home for the past twelve years, but it was time to move on. Carefully, he pulled his notebooks from a drawer and removed the holographic generator. Without the hologram, the book-lined shelves disappeared. The interior of the room changed from an elaborate office to a modern day bedroom.

He activated the secret panel in the wall revealing his laboratory. The door whispered closed behind him.

He engaged the locking mechanism to secure the facility, then turned on the remote generator and powered up the machine which looked like an old-fashioned tanning bed. Unless one knew how to operate it, it would be of no use. His plans were to use it now and for that reason, he needed it secure. It opened a portal which must remain open until the end of his journey. He knew where he would go next.

After securing the notebooks and generator within the laboratory, he opened a closet. Inside, arranged in chronological order, was clothing representing centuries of Earth fashion. He had successfully travelled back and forth in time, chasing down errors in judgements that had led to the problems that plagued man in a future time. Davo Fost was a perfectionist. Each suit of clothing was expertly made and labelled with its relevant time period. Each item was in ready order for travel on a moment's notice, though he never haphazardly engaged the machine. Every movement was well-thought out and planned. Every intersection between one time and another was selected so as not to disrupt the time continuum, but now he was on the brink of doing just that.

Carefully, he removed his solar suit, detaching the oxygen generator and arranged it on the hanger. Stepping out of the gravity boots, he replaced them with brown wing tip shoes. To complete his ensemble he dressed in gabardine slacks, a white long-sleeved shirt, a broad blue stripped tie and a tweed jacket. The final details required a trip to the bathroom, where he shaved off his beard, cut his hair, dabbing sable brown hair dye to his temples. He removed the green contact lenses and set a pair of aviator frames on his nose. He smiled, satisfied with his reflection. He was going back to the end of the twentieth century. This was the timeframe where pharmaceuticals changed humanity, and he wanted to know why.

He was going back to deter man from setting in motion those actions that would put an end to mankind. It was clearly there in the DNA samples he had meticulously collected. Toward the end of the twentieth century something changed, and then in the twenty-first century it was aggravated and changed again. It might have gone on for thousands of generations without the adverse effects, but an accelerant was introduced which rendered humanity infertile in less than two hundred years. It was the catalyst that befuddled him. Was it the result of chemical warfare? Why was there nothing in the historical records?

His stay in this time was ending poorly. The mechanical whir kicked into a high-pitched whine, the lights flickered. Davo gulped down a flask of blue viscous liquid, then lay down on the bed and secured the lid. The lights flickered and went out. The whine continued for another minute, then clicked off.

As the guards entered, they called out and searched. There was no sign of Davo Fost, no remnants of the twelve years he had lived here. One guard who had often visited, scratched his head in confusion, nothing looked like he remembered.

DIAMONDS

Diamonds sparkling in the sunshine. Millions of them. All sizes and shapes. My eyes delight in the twinkling, but soon I realize what I am looking at. Not diamonds.

* * *

It's May and one thing after another has kept me from my garden and getting my yard ready for Summer. Yesterday I pulled the patio furniture onto the deck and washed away the winter grime, gently reflecting the life I've lived with this table and six chairs.

In another lifetime, we bought it at Costco, found someone with a truck to cart it home, then gave it years of use in our sunroom as our breakfast table. A place where the boys and I ate, read the newspaper, and worried over homework assignments.

I could not leave it behind and packed it up to make the move north. I had one crew to pack the truck and another to unpack it. As the second crew pulled the mattresses off the truck, I remembered and warned that the glass tabletop was wedged between the mattresses. It seemed to float through the air, but we caught it. And it survived sixteen winters here.

A little soap and water washed away the grime, but

as soon as I shut off the water, raindrops fell from the sky. I hastened back indoors. It rained all day.

Today dawned sunny and bright, and I picked up the task. I fluffed each of the chair cushions and tied them to the chairs. I unfurled the new patio umbrella and set it in the table. The umbrella's bright red and orange colors picked up the blooms in the wildflower garden. After sweeping the deck, I suggested we eat dinner outdoors tonight.

Inside, reading the last chapter in my book, I heard a noise. Looking outside the umbrella lay tossed by the wind, and I looked to the table. Beneath the table was now the pile of glimmering diamonds. As in some fairytale, Rumpelstiltskin made a trade. Leaving diamonds in place of a glass tabletop. My need to set the umbrella, and the wind that rose this afternoon, reduced the once sturdy glass sheet to shards.

It was not only a patio table, but a bridge that spanned my life before and after. A new table is on its way. A bucket of diamonds waits to be recycled.

What's Lurking In The Pantry?

Three children huddled in front of the open pantry. On the shelf were several boxes of breakfast cereal. Usually they push and shove one another trying to be first. But this morning, they hold back, staring into the cupboard.

"It must be Tony the tiger," five-year-old Lucy said.

"No, Count Chocula. He's a vampire," seven-year-old Jack argued.

"I think it could be them," four-year-old Mark said pointing to the blue box.

"Them? No way," Jack said.

"But there's three of 'em."

"How about the Captain? He's a pirate, and he's got a sword?" Lucy said.

The three faces looked from one box to another. Who was it? The tiger, the captain, the vampire, or Snap, Crackle and Pop?

"What's holding you up. Pick your cereal. Let's get going," Mom said.

They turned from the pantry in one movement.

"Could we have waffles?" Jack asked.

"Pancakes," said Lucy clapping her hands.

Their mother looked at them. "But you always have cereal." She expected them to grab a box, and sit down like usual, but they stood looking at her, expectantly.

"Jack get the waffles out of the freezer. Lucy, set the table. We've got to get a move on."

The children followed her orders and as the waffles popped out of the toaster, they sat at the table and ate.

"So, which one is it?" Mark whispered.

Lucy looked at her brothers, "Does mom know?"

"I still think it's Count Chocula or that leprechaun. He's a tricky guy."

For several days the breakfast routine was upset. Instead of each child taking their preferred cereal from the pantry and eating, they asked for something other than cereal. One morning it was waffles, another scrambled eggs, another pizza. Lucy always wanted pancakes. Their mother wondered what happened with the cereal. Usually the thrill of waiting for the toy to fall out was enough to keep them eating. Now not one, but all three seemed uninterested. She opened and tasted each of the cereals checking to see if they were stale. No, the same sugary sweet as when she was a girl

That night at bedtime, Lucy said her prayers. "God bless Mommy, Daddy, Jack and Mark." She let out a deep breath. "And please tell me who the cereal killer is so that I can eat Fruit Loops again."

Her mother stifled a giggle and kissed her good night.

Behind the closed bedroom door, she let loose with a laugh. "You won't believe this."

Her husband looked up from the book he was reading. "What?"

The kids must have heard the news about that serial killer and now they won't eat cereal."

The next morning, the dad sat down at the breakfast table with five boxes of cereal in front of him. The kids were surprised to see their father there so late in the morning.

"Dad, be careful," Lucy warned. "One of them is a killer."

Mark sucked in his breath, then popped his thumb into his mouth.

Jack stood to his father's left. "Dad, do you know which one it is?"

"It's one we don't eat, so there is nothing to worry about. I heard they caught the killer and gave him Life."

Bowls and spoons clanged as the kids sat down and the family breakfast routine returned to normal.

DINNER CONVERSATION

Barbara stumbles through the door and drops her purse on the table.

"Bad day?" I call from the kitchen.

"Really bad day. I'm gonna pour me a drink. You want one too?"

"Sure, babe. Dinner should be ready in a few."

I hear the clink of the glasses and the sound of liquid splashing into them. *Is she pouring straight bourbon?* Must've been a really bad shift. People know cops get it bad, but the 9-1-1 operators sometimes get it just as bad.

I toss the salad and hum a tune, giving her decompression time. I know she needs it when she comes home like this.

Ten minutes later, I set the table and call out that dinner is ready.

She sets her glass, now only half full, on the table and places one for me.

We say grace, hand in hand. Some traditions keep the sanity. She takes a bite of salad, and I know she's ready to talk.

"I got a call right away. It was a woman, near hysterics, said her name was Nancy. Someone was missing. Nancy was crying. I tried to calm her. It was her father. Nancy sat him down with breakfast and jumped into the shower. 'Five minutes' she said, 'I was out of the room for only five minutes.' When she came back, he was gone."

Barbara blinks back tears and sighs, like it's her own story. This one got to her. Her dad's in a home for dementia patients. We visit, but he doesn't know her anymore. Asks about her but doesn't recognize her. It's getting harder to watch.

Her salad finished, she reaches for the bowl of broccoli, then helps herself to a chicken breast.

"Seems he wanted to find his dog. It was a Lab, named Skip, he had as a boy – in his mind that dog's been gone minutes, not decades. I get her dad's description, he was wearing a light blue short-sleeve shirt, blue jeans, and red bedroom slippers and maybe a green baseball cap, she couldn't be sure. 'He's 73,' Nancy said, 'but thinks it's still 1950.' I get the address and send dispatch."

Bourbon sloshes in the glasses when Barbara slams her fork on the table. "That's the thing. I don't know what priority they give it. I don't know when they go out, or even if they do help this woman find her father. Nancy had already been up and down the block before she called."

"Honey…"

Her look tells me she doesn't need me calming her down. She needs to run through the whole event. Blow off steam. I get up and bring the bourbon bottle to the table.

She nods, then eats in silence for a while.

"I got another call toward the end of my shift. Another woman screaming, said her name was Shirley. She was yelling 'There's a man breaking into my house. He's coming in through the back door. I told him I got a gun.' I get her address and alert the police to a burglary in process."

She takes a bite of chicken and chews it like she's counting the number of chews, then washes it down with bourbon.

"I ask Shirley if she's alone. 'No, I got my Lab, Duke, but he's no watchdog.' She tries to describe the burglar, says she only sees his head, one hand. Then Shirley starts yelling at the man to get out. I ask her if he's leaving. She says no but that he keeps saying something only she can't tell what it is. I'm confused by the fact that he's breaking in her door, but she only sees his hand and his head. I'm trying to figure this out, when there's the sound of gunfire. 'I shot him, I done it,' Shirley said."

"I can't hear anything. I ask if she can hear the police siren? She says no, but my screen shows that car two-twelve is arriving at the address. I tell Shirley to set the gun down. Ask about the man. She says he's lying on the floor, blood everywhere. Then I hear a police officer say something to her. The phone goes dead."

Barbara finishes her bourbon. She takes a piece of bread, wipes up the gravy on her plate, but she doesn't eat it. She sets it down and pushes the plate away.

I can tell that isn't the end yet.

"As I'm getting ready to leave work, I hear on the dispatch that the would-be burglar was coming in through the dog door. Apparently following the dog from the street. She shot him in the head. He's dead. I knew then what he was saying when the woman was screaming at him. He was calling 'Skip.'"

Do It Yourself – Gone Bad

Don is a kind-hearted well-meaning guy, with an exaggerated view of his DIY talent.

When he was between jobs, his wife, Kim, suggested that he keep busy doing odd jobs around the house. She was thinking of cutting the lawn on a regular basis and taking over weeding the flower beds. He thought about a kitchen remodel.

As an accountant for a local aerospace company, he did a fine job, filled in the forms in the proper places and mailed in the reports in a timely manner. Being handy with tools other than a ten-key calculator was not his forte.

Kim came home from her job as a grocery store checker on Monday and found a pile of large boxes in the living room of their suburban ranch-style home.

"What's this, Don?" she asked.

"I'm redoing the kitchen," he said.

"What are you talking about?"

"You said I should make myself useful." Don affected a wide-legged stance, holding a power drill in one hand and a hammer in the other, his empty tool belt hung from his hips.

"In the yard, Don. Not in my kitchen." Kim walked around the boxes and headed for the kitchen.

Don tried to block her. "You keep complaining about how you don't have enough light. I'm putting in fluorescent lights."

"You mean like shop lights?" She bent over reading the contents of the boxes.

"No, I'm gonna make you a nice suspended ceiling like the Ford's next door. They just redid their whole kitchen. I think we can accomplish the same thing by updating the lighting. We've got nice cabinets..."

Kim nodded and stood looking at her kitchen. "Don, how can you do a drop ceiling when our cabinets go all the way to the ceiling. You've got no room to drop anything?"

"No worries, I got it all worked out."

"But..."

Kim had second and third thoughts about what Don was going to do. After all she still had the bathroom door fiasco to contend with. The last time Don was laid off, he decided to tile the bathroom floor. He studied up on it, and enrolled in a workshop at the local hardware store. Then he purchased tile, adhesive, and grout. He rented a tile cutter and got to work. His efforts paid off, the tile was laid in straight rows, the grout lined up. He took the time to remove the toilet, tile under it and replace the wax seal before resetting it. All in all, it looked like a professional job. He repainted the floor molding and put it back in place. For nearly a week though, the bathroom door stood in the dining room while he worked. When he rehung the door it would not clear the new floor. The tile was higher than the old linoleum, in fact, Don had tiled over the existing floor.

"Not to worry," Don said. "I'll just sand some off the bottom."

Then the door lay across two saw horses and Don sanded the bottom of the door, but it still did not clear the tile.

"I've got it now," he said when he came back from the hardware store with a planer, "This will take off that pesky quarter inch."

Only this did not seem to make much difference. Kim watched him from the doorway as he re-planed the door again, shavings dropping to the dining room floor.

When the door still hit the tile, he stomped into the kitchen and removed a beer from the refrigerator. He scratched his head and took more measurements.

Kim heard him swear, the refrigerator door slam again, followed by the sound of the electric circular saw.

"Whoa, what are you doing?" Kim asked running into the dining room.

Don shut off the saw and looked at her, "I'm fixing it, now back off."

Kim did back off—all the way to the garden where she dropped to her knees and weeded the flowerbeds.

Later, she found Don asleep on the couch, and the bathroom door hung. Gingerly, she opened it and it easily cleared the tile floor. She nodded in appreciation. He had done the job. For a time it seemed like he wasn't going to be able to finish it. As she closed the door she noted a shaft of light through the two-inch gap at the top of the door. Puzzled, she opened and closed the door several times before she realized that he had been shaving off the top not the bottom of the door. She didn't say anything to Don, but she started watching the ads for an interior door sale.

What sort of a mess was he going to make of her kitchen?

Kim thought Don agreed to return the lighting and not give her the aforementioned dropped ceiling. But when she came home from work, she found that was not so. The metal framing was installed with the ceiling covered with fluorescent lighting boxes. He was installing the frosted ceiling tiles as she watched.

"Don, I thought we agreed…"

Don hummed a tune which Kim did not recognize.

"Just look," she said as she walked under the ladder and touched the corner of one of the upper cabinet doors. "See, it won't open…"

The door swung open revealing the glassware.

"I thought…" she said as she checked the next cabinet and the next. Each time the door swung easily. She stepped back and tried to figure out how he had got the drop ceiling in, when the cabinet doors had gone all the way to the ceiling.

"I told you not to worry. I took care of everything." Don set the last ceiling tile in place and climbed down from the ladder. "Honey, I got it covered. Look at all this light."

Kim was still swinging doors and looking. "For crying out loud, you cut the cabinet doors!"

"You never use those top shelves anyway. Besides if you had to get into one of them you can always do it by removing the ceiling tile."

That was the last DIY job Kim allowed Don to undertake. She sold all his tools for a dollar at a garage sale when he went fishing.

AFTERWARD

There are so many things wrong with this picture. Only I can't name them. It is like one of those hidden pictures. Find the fourteen dogs, but there are no dogs. Only cats. Or I perceive them as cats, but my word for cat is "bowl of cereal."

You point the dogs out to me. You say, "See there, and there, and there. You see them, now don't you?"

There is so much hope in your voice. I nod. I don't see the dogs and I don't know what you point to. I turn away.

You hold the picture closer to my face, your voice is louder. "Do you see the dog?" You speak slowly. It sounds like "D-ooo y-ooo s-eee?"

I am not deaf, I am not blind. I can see but I can't find the correct words to communicate with you. I am lost but right here. It is frustrating to be me.

"Tired," I say. It is tried and true. You fluff my pillow, cover me with a blanket and leave me alone for a time.

"Sleep," you say.

I close my eyes until I hear the door shut. Now, I'm alone. Only not in peace. Questions swirl in my mind, go around and round. There are no answers, no anchors to hold my focus. Everything is not as it should be. I do not know what was before, but nothing feels right.

I don't understand what happened to me. This is not how it was before. But I have no memory of before. "Traumatic Brain Injury," they explain, but I do not understand. I was somewhere else, then I was here. What happened I want to ask, but my words tumble out wrong. "Ice cream," I said once and they laughed nervously. Their staring eyes tell me that I have done it wrong, said it wrong, that I am acting wrong. I try to get it right, but I am tired of not knowing. The woman who sits beside my bed bites her nails.

I sleep.

There is a blank space between my questions and now. It is dark outside where it was light. This seems significant but I cannot say why. I hear footsteps, the door creaks open and someone looks in. I close my eyes and lay still waiting for them to go away. It is better here than the other place. That place was full of noises, and wires and tubes. I was controlled by all the machinery, and I knew that was wrong. What were they doing to me?

The woman is sitting beside me when I wake. She is the one person I know. I know she is supposed to be here with me. She is someone who has been in my life, someone who has protected me. Her eyes tell me she is afraid for me; tears streak her face.

"Groundhog," I say.

"Good morning Sweetie," she says, a smile erases the worry that was there. "Do you want to try some breakfast today?"

"Lawnmower," I say. I am confident that this time I used the right word. Her face tells me that I did not. She smiles through her confusion and helps me sit up. She props pillows behind me, and the smell of her skin is familiar, comforting.

"Oatmeal," she says and holds a bowl in her hand. She dips the spoon into the creamy porridge and brings the spoon to my lips.

I recognize that she is feeding me, I am hungry, but something sets off an alarm within me. I cannot control the reaction. I throw up my hands, knocking the spoon away. I scream. The sound is piercing and frightens me. She remains calm. Sets the bowl down and begins to sing a song, a lullaby. I close my eyes and a wave of calm envelopes me. I curl into a fetal position, laying on my right side I bring my knees to my chest. I heard this music a long time ago. All will be well as long as she sings to me.

A DOOR LEFT OPEN

It was because of the door left open that the cat ran out of the house. At first, content with its escape, it sat on the lawn preening. Then it chased a squawking crow up a tree in a neighboring yard.

Because the cat climbed the tree, it sat mewing on the branch after the bird flew away. The cat appeared to be waiting to be rescued. Because the cat sat in the tree, crows cawed, screeching at the intruder. This noise alerted two black Labs sniffing about the street. They detected the cat in the tree and started barking.

Eloise Davis resided in the house near the tree now inhabited by the cat. She heard the barking dogs. Being afraid of dogs, she called a neighbor for help.

"Whose dogs?" Bill Brown, the neighbor asked.

"Why are they barking at my tree?" Eloise asked.

Bill Brown tried to help. He approached the dogs with pepper spray but found the dogs friendly. They wagged their tales and sniffed his pockets for treats. When they stopped barking, he heard the cat.

"Whose cat?" he asked.

By now Alice Stuart and her sister Mary had come outside next door and looked into the tree at the cat. Because the cat was a housecat, no one recognized it.

"Whose cat?" they asked in unison as sisters are

likely to do.

"Get a ladder," Alice said.

"Call the fire department," Mary said.

As the onlookers grew in number, the owner of the cat, Marge Black, looked out her window. "What's going on?" she asked. When she found her front door open, she realized her cat had escaped.

"Help," she called from the doorway.

Several of the neighbors hurried over to her.

"What's wrong?" Bill Brown asked.

"Call 9-1-1," Mary said.

"My cat is missing," Marge said.

At that moment, a fire truck pulled onto the street, sirens blaring. Two police cruisers followed. Then came the local television station news van. Firemen jumped from the truck and unwound hoses. The captain addressed the crowd, "Where's the fire?"

"No fire," said Bill Brown.

"No fire?" repeated the fireman.

"It's a cat," Alice Stuart said pointing up the tree.

"A cat?" the firemen said in unison.

"The cat is stuck in the tree."

As every eye peered up into the tree, the black and white cat clambered down, jumped onto the walkway and confidently walked home, entering through the door left open.

THE DRESS

Six-year-old Tommy cast an eye into his mother's closet and saw a fancy dress. He did not know about bridesmaid dresses or style.

Some years before my sister, Joan was asked to be the matron of honor for a young friend. "Don't worry," the bride-to-be told her, "I've got all the dresses." Joan had two young children then and didn't have time to worry. Two weeks before the wedding a large box arrived. Inside was her maid of honor dress. In tears, she phoned me.

"Oh my god," she said, "It's a Little Boo Peep dress."

"It can't be that bad," I said.

"It is!" she said.

"Does it fit?"

"I guess so, but it's so horrible! It has a hoop skirt and big puffy sleeves…"

"Oh no." I couldn't think what else to say.

"And a bonnet!

"A what?"

"A bonnet, like Boo Peep."

"You could get the flu and miss the wedding?" I offered.

She wore the dress and the bonnet. The wedding was a fairy tale event. Afterward the dress, along with the hoop skirt, was relegated to the back of her closet and forgotten.

* * *

When Tommy was six, he lost his first tooth. He soon learned about leaving the tooth under his pillow and waking to find what the tooth fairy left in its place. During that summer, he soon had a full mouth of missing teeth and dimes jingled in his piggy bank. Many of his friends were also losing their baby teeth.

What Tommy didn't know was that Joan was pregnant with another child.. That summer the kids were home from school, and they had day camp and soccer and Little League. One had to be somewhere for practice, another had a game across town. Joan often felt like a cab driver moving the boys from one place to another and had little time to watch them play. Joan was run ragged. She re-instated nap time so she could get some rest. Tommy complained, he wasn't a baby that needed a nap. She explained to him that she was the one who was tired, she needed it.

The last week of summer vacation was busier than usual with buying school clothes and supplies. The first day of school finally arrived, and the boys were out of the house. Joan eased into a chair and sighed her relief.

But in the first week of school, she was sent to the principal's office. It was Tommy's teacher who wanted to see her. Joan took her seat in the outer office and waited. She pondered that in all her years at school she had never been called to the principal's office, her mother had never been called there because of her behavior.

"Come in, Joan." Mr. Williams said as he held the door open for her.

"Good morning," she said. "What has Tommy done?

"No problem, just thought you might like to know what your son said about you."

"What?" She didn't know what to think. If he hadn't done anything wrong, why was she here?

"It seems that Tommy stood up in class yesterday and told everyone to stop bothering his mother. He said you were too tired to work every night. When everyone looked at him, he told them they had to stop losing their teeth.

At first they laughed at him, but he explained. "I saw it. She has the dress, you know with the big skirt and it's all sparkly." He nodded, "My mother is the tooth fairy."

Even Steven

My uncle Steven was a finicky bachelor with a kind heart. He remembered each of his nieces and nephews, always sending a birthday card with a crisp two-dollar bill inside. Every birthday, every year.

I was not close to him, but after my father passed, I felt a need to keep in touch. On a visit to his home, he confided that if he penny-pinched he would be able to support himself without need of any charity. I looked around at his sparsely decorated trailer and nodded, thinking to myself that I could never be content to live as he did. It was neat and clean, but nothing was purchased new, all second or third hand. I'd planned to take him out for a meal, but he refused, offering instead to heat up leftovers for me. I looked into the container he fetched from the refrigerator and smiled. Mac and cheese with cut-up hot dogs. "Yum," I lied, my fingers crossed behind my back.

Over that meal he told me he wanted to live "Even Steven." He wanted to live long enough to use his funds, and not a day longer. He asked me to be the "executioner of his state." I knew what he meant and did not embarrass him by correcting. He handed me a well-worn copy of his will and advised that there wasn't much to fuss about.

* * *

Over the next years, I visited him once or twice a year. Until I received a call from his neighbor, Bill. Steven had gone peacefully in his sleep the night before. Bill knew that Steven wanted me to take care of things. I called the funeral home and made arrangements. Steven had prepaid his cremation years before. He left no detail overlooked.

One by one I made contact with the rest of his relatives, all his nieces and nephews, and we agreed to meet for a family service. Steven hadn't wanted to obligate anyone, but we wanted to repay his thoughtfulness, a lifetime of those two-dollar bills arriving in our mailboxes.

I began the task of contacting his creditors and closing out his accounts.

As if by design, I found that his financial cache had dwindled to less than five hundred dollars, enough to pay the trailer park rent for another month. At the bank, the teller reminded me about his safety deposit box. Inside were eight envelopes addressed to the nieces and nephews, our birthday cards for the coming year, complete with the crisp two-dollar bills.

Steven had only one credit card in his wallet. When I called to cancel, they reported that he had a current balance due of fifty-six dollars and twenty-eight cents; however, it was a cash rewards card and there was a credit of fifty-six dollars and twenty cents. The representative chuckled. "We'll take care of that eight-cent difference," she said. Then added, "Please accept our condolences on the loss of your uncle."

And that was that. There were no outstanding debts, the balance of his bank account and personal belongings were turned over to Bill as the will spelled out.

Uncle Steven lived his one hundred and one years as he wanted, and in the end everything evened out.

FAR BETTER OR WORSE

Astrid Moncrief sat in the chair as if it might be to her death. Admitting to a hearing loss due to age was as outrageous as wearing flannel pjs in public. She was thankful when they shut the door to the exam room, appreciating privacy while she ate her humble pie. A smile crossed her lips at the thought. The attendant mumbled instructions which Astrid could not hear. How long had she been living this lie? For years she smiled and laughed pantomiming her reply, having no idea what the conversation was about. Things would surely be different with hearing aids.

The attendant fussed over Astrid's ears, moving her hair, pushing the contraption behind each ear. Without so much as a snap, crackle or pop, Astrid heard every word the attendant spoke. Her eyes opened wide. Her mouth broke into a smile. It was amazing. Astrid vowed to never take them off, never turn down the volume, and to the devil with trying to hide the fact she wore them. She would hear everything, even sounds she didn't like, horns honking in traffic, and dreadful music teenagers listened to.

"I can hear. I can really hear," Astrid said.

Smiling, the attendant instructed her on the volume controls and how to change the batteries. Astrid memorized all she needed to know.

"Another happy customer," the attendant said as Astrid left.

* * *

Outside, Astrid didn't fret over the wait for her ride because she could hear birds singing high in the trees across the street. She marveled at how harmonious the world was and dismayed that she had waited so long.

The driver pulled up and opened the door for Astrid. She settled herself into the seat, listening to strains of music. Abruptly there was a snap snap sound. It wasn't from the radio. Astrid realized the sound came from the driver. "What are you doing?" she asked.

"What do you mean?" he said.

"That snap snap, what is it?"

"Snap snap? I don't know what you are talking about."

No sooner had he spoken, than she heard the sound again.

"That sound!" Astrid said.

"It's gum. I used to smoke, but I gave it up. I started eating candy and gained twenty pounds, so now I am chewing gum to not eat or smoke."

"Oh," she said. "Here's my stop."

* * *

At home, she told Frank how much better she felt because she could hear.

"What? What's that you say?"

"I can hear," she said.

"Who's here?" he said, looking around.

"Dinner is ready," Astrid said taking their plates to the table.

Frank picked up his glass of tea. "Slurp, gulp, gulp."

Astrid looked at him. "Are you doing that on purpose?"

"What?" He forked a bite of chicken.

She wondered, *was I as bad as Frank before the hearing aids? How long did I ignore my hearing loss? When did I quit saying "What?" At least a year ago, I began smiling, nodding, and following what those around me were doing.*

Astrid shook her head at these memories.

"What?" Frank muttered looking at her. He took another bite of food.

"Crunch, crunch, crunch."

"Really?" she said laying her fork down.

Frank looked up. "What?"

"You're a very noisy eater. I never noticed before."

Frank shrugged and bit into his garlic bread.

"Crunch, chomp, chomp, chomp."

Astrid shook her head and put her hands over her ears. She turned down the volume on the hearing aids, down to where she could no longer hear him chewing, slurping and crunching.

Then he belched.

She watched his mouth open and close, but she did not hear it. "Better, much better."

"Butter, you want the butter?"

"What?" Oh drat! I turned off the hearing aids, now he is talking to me again.

Later they watched a favorite television program.

"Frank, turn the volume down." She adjusted her own volume. *It's amazing the neighbors don't complain, it's so loud.* For the first time, she understood the dialog between the characters, making her wonder why she enjoyed the show. When Frank laughed, she had laughed with him, but then she had no idea what the characters were saying. Now that she heard them, she no longer cared.

At bedtime, the cat curled beside her. It purred as she stroked its back. Astrid smiled realizing she had not heard that sound in some time. "Life's a lot better," she sighed.

Astrid awoke in the middle of a nightmare. She was being chased by a bulldozer or a tank. She couldn't relate how those thoughts came into her head. Frank snorted in sleep and she recognized it as the sound of the tank as it belched smoke bearing down on her.

She jostled Frank, shook her head and took out the hearing aids. Placing them gently on the nightstand, she thought, *I guess there are some things I don't need to hear.*

UNCLE JACK

In my youth, my Uncle Jack seemed larger than life. He'd suddenly appear on the front porch and ring the bell. Mother said something under her breath when she saw him. Dad slunk away to the barn rather than shake his hand.

Jack didn't seem to care. He'd pull things out of his pockets for us kids. A roll of life savers that he'd parcel out one at a time, all the while spinning yarns about where he'd been, what he'd seen. Sometimes he had souvenirs from his travels and would tell us about faraway places. He claimed to have ridden an elephant, and a camel, and fought a crocodile. Uncle Jack was a real live hero. We provided an enraptured audience. We never questioned the authenticity of what he said, even when it conflicted with what he had told us before. He claimed to have been in the Army and had war stories to share, until one day he told us about being at sea with the Navy.

When my brother asked about pirates, Uncle Jack claimed that once he'd been on a pirate ship. Father glared at him from across the room, then cleared his throat. That sound made me pull back from the story, be sure I was sitting up straight, elbows off the table. Father ruled us with those guttural sounds, no shouting.

Later, Jack would sit with Father at his desk and sip whiskey. They spoke in low tones; we couldn't hear what they said. Then Jack would pick me up and swing me around pretending I was an airplane. He'd tickle Bobby and the baby – then he'd leave as quickly as he arrived.

Years later I learned the reason behind Uncle Jack's visits. He needed money, and Dad always helped his brother. Uncle Jack had a hard life, spent time in jail for writing bad checks, sold items of questionable ownership. That was how Dad put it.

Uncle Jack hasn't dropped by in a long time. Mom cried and Dad said it was better this way. They never explained it to me or Bobby. We liked to think that he was back on the pirate ship or flying an airplane around the world. Even still, when there was a knock at the door, we'd race to see if it is Uncle Jack.

FOUND

A stranger tapped me on the shoulder. I turned in my seat to see a middle-aged man in a three-piece suit sitting across the aisle.

"Is that your bag?" he asked pointing.

I looked down to see a green canvas bag that lay partially under my seat.

"No," I said.

"It's moving," he said.

We both looked at the bag. It was a grocery tote, and it was indeed wiggling.

Mid-afternoon, the subway car was not crowded. The seat behind me was unoccupied as were the two in front of me. The man sat across the aisle surrounded by empty seats. I looked around. There seemed to be no one watching. I pulled the bag from under the seat, and peered in. Of course, I wanted to know what was inside, but also, if there was any identification of the owner.

Inside was a newborn baby swaddled tightly in a bright pink blanket. The baby, a girl, I presumed, stretched her arms, and kicked her legs unwrapping the blanket. She was waking up, about to make her presence heard.

The man and I exchanged looks of surprise and scanned again the other passengers. No one seemed to be watching what we were doing. The car came to a stop and the man and I rose. Was it our stop or were we fleeing the responsibility for the baby? At the last second, I picked up the tote bag, looping the handles over my arm, and stepped out onto the platform.

GAMBIT

I missed the Gamer's Convention, aka "The Con" last year so I psyched myself up for it this year. My friends reminisced about a game they participated in the year before and suggested I consider it. I jumped at the chance, wanting to fit in. This wasn't my first con, but I desired some shared history with this group of friends. This year The Con was held at the Crescent Hotel, taking over all the ballrooms and meeting rooms. The halls were filled with die hard gamers and cos players in costumes. Based on their recommendation, I went in search of the game.

"The rules of the game are organic," Kellie warned.

"Go to the game room and sign up to play. You'll be dealt a player card, and given instruction," Paul added.

"The costumes are amazing. It'll blow your mind," Susan said.

A red-bearded young man hastily whispered the rules of the game in the darkened hallway after he dealt me a card. "Show your card only when you suspect another player in proximity. Find the players. Find the playing field, and jump in."

"What?" I said stepping back. "Are you serious?" Asking was a waste of time. He turned and vanished.

A brunette cheerleader stepped in front of me. The

teenaged girl carried an eight by ten laminated card tucked under her arm as if it mandated authority. I wondered if she was a part of the game. The card I was dealt, "Liberty For All" was concealed under my jacket. It seemed identical to the one the cheerleader carried.

Not sure what my next step should be, I decided to follow the cheerleader. She was moving fast, and I had to double time to catch up. She turned the corner and floated down a stairway. I was on her tail. A figure of speech. She did not have an actual tail as far as I could see, but other con goers we passed did have tails and ears, some had horns, more than two in one case. The costumes at these events fascinated me. Many were hand-made, but some were designed and sewn by serious fabricators. Imagination was what it was all about.

"Wait," I wanted to call out, but I needed to verify that she was in the game. Maybe she'd lead me to other players, maybe to the game.

After three flights, she stepped into a hallway and stopped at a door. She opened it after a quick rap, then flashed the card to someone inside and exited. I positioned myself to see her card, "Five Minutes," it read. She repeated this process down the hallway, eleven times in all. Each time in the exact sequence. No one joined up. *Was she as new to this as me? Was I supposed to flash my card as well?*

She stopped, turned and faced me in the empty hallway. I almost collided with her.

"Are you following me?" she demanded in a husky growl.

"Yes," I admitted.

"Do I know you?" Her brown eyes bore into mine.

"Er," I stuttered and pulled out my card showing it to her.

"Oh," she said. "You're one of them."

I stepped back. *Isn't she one of us? Have I erred in proclaiming my play?*

"Wait here," she said touching my arm gently, and darted around the corner.

I waited five minutes. Just like her card said, if that mattered. Behind me the doors opened, and people poured out of the rooms, surrounding me as they made their way through the hall. I circled watching them for signs. I feared the cheerleader wasn't coming back. *Would she send other players to me? Am I being duped? Really, why do I want to be into this stupid game?*

Suddenly, I realized the connection between her sign and the people spilling into the halls. She was a timekeeper, not a player. My spirits fell. I began to shuffle my way back to the main hall of The Con.

A door slammed, and I heard heavy footfalls behind me. I turned to find a seven-foot giant advancing toward me. At my full height, I barely reached his chest. He was dressed in animal skins and looked like a Neanderthal. The skins were real because as he neared, the they stunk of decay and sweat.

"Ew!" I cried. My eyes burned from the stench. He reached inside his furry shroud and flashed a card, "Missing Link."

"Oh," I said.

He looked at me, a twinkle of surprise in his eyes, then he bowed formally from the waist.

Now what?

He motioned for me to follow and turned back the way he had come.

I smirked; he lumbered as you might suspect an actual Neanderthal would. I thought he played his part to the hilt. What should I be doing in my role? Where would I get a costume? I followed keeping a respectable distance so that I could breathe.

Back down the corridor, around the corner and into the stairwell. Down one floor, then another. Wooden planks replaced the cement steps, creaking under the weight of the Neanderthal.

Another floor down and the fluorescent lights switched to torch-like sconces unless they were actual torches. Black smoke smudged the walls above them showing me they were real.

I questioned why I was following this ape-like giant – only because he had a card? Was he the missing link for me to join the game? *Is this the game? What's ahead? Should I turn back?*

Voltar or Sasquatch, whoever he was, thudded through a doorway and into a dark corridor. I followed. He didn't check to see if I was still behind him but trudged ahead. The torch lights flickered as he passed. Then the lights went out.

"Oy," I cried. Another door slammed. It was metal and heavy; there was a definite clank when it shut behind me. I shuddered.

"Hello?" I called out. "Anyone?" I felt my heart thumping. For a moment, I heard other sounds, human or animal; I was uncertain. I could not be sure if they were cries of anger, fear, or triumph. Those sounds swirled around me in the darkness. A cold shiver ran down my spine. Fear gripped me. *What have I gotten myself into?*

Switching to survival mode, I threw up my hands in surrender. A dim light flickered overhead. *What's that?* I waited and watched. It happened whenever I raised my arms. I repeated the action, hands overhead and again there was a faint glimmer. *Did I do that?* I lifted my left arm alone. Nothing. I tried my right arm, holding it high. And there was a light, brightening as if there were a flashlight in my hand, but only when my hand was elevated. *What's this?*

In the dim light, I saw that I was penned in a cell complete with bars. Quickly I shouted, "Liberty for All," figuring that if this was part of the game, that was my card.

I heard a click, and the door swung free. With my right hand held high, I hurried down the corridor looking for the door back to the stairwell. I was hell-bent on getting out of there. I had enough. I couldn't remember how many flights I descended, but I would be happy to see florescent lights again. I heard the sounds of other people but ignored it, determined to get out of there. I opened the door.

The room was fully lit, and the Neanderthal sat at a table among other costumed players. There was Wonder Woman, Snow White, a Jedi, a Storm Trooper, the Doctor, and a spat-shoed Mr. Peanut. I hadn't seen him in years. But right in front of me was the most beautiful costume. A woman dressed as the Statue of Liberty, her face burnished copper, a torch in her right hand, and the elaborate folds of her tarnished green gown. Mr. Peanut interrupted my gaze when he yelled, "Quit primping in front of that mirror. Take your seat, Lady Liberty, it's your turn."

I looked back to the woman and realized I was viewing my reflection. *Where did this costume come from? Is it a hologram?* I shrugged off my concerns, stood taller. Then I took my seat at the table. Gaming was never before this thrilling.

- - - - - - - - - ADVERTISEMENT - - - - - - - - -

The Federal Food and Drug Administration along with the pharmaceutical company responsible for Ritalin, announced today the release of a new drug that will make writers sit up and take note.

Do you suffer from Writer's Attention Deficit Disorder?
No? Really, think about it. Do you start stories and never finish? Do you leave characters in the middle of a mystery, adventure, or love triangle without resolution? If you have unfinished work you may suffer from Writer's Attention Deficit Disorder, or WADD.

Do you sit pen in hand, or fingers hovering over the keyboard, yet no words come?
That is writer's block, a common symptom of WADD.

Does your inner critic make you cringe?

Don't despair.
Don't line your pockets with rocks and wade into the river. Pick up the phone, or log online, and order today. This product is being sold directly to suffering writers. You won't find it on the shelves at CVS or Rexall Drug, you need to buy it direct.
The product is WRITALIN, the miracle supplement to get you up and writing
Say goodbye to that inner critic!

Proven Results!

Studies conducted with successful authors known for producing volumes of work (S.K.-you know who we mean) show that the key ingredient in WRITALIN naturally occurs in only a few individuals. This has been extracted, studied, and genetically enhanced to produce the astounding results of WRITALIN.

Now available in two strengths

The normal strength will strengthen the resolve of any writer working on a full-length book or novel. Half doses are prescribed for poets, short story writers, and essayists. The extra strength formula contains an additional extract which is recommended for authors hell-bent on trilogies. Proper dosing is advised. One playwright working on a one act play, took the extra strength formula and produced a thirteen-hour one act play. Improper dosing may result in an increased imagination, be it fantasy or horror. Writers suffering from this side effect longer than eight hours are encouraged to seek medical attention immediately.

Endorsements

"I started so many stories but could never keep my characters straight … until Writalin. Now I've gone from one book to many and … jumped genres." *Ms. J.K.R.*

"After thousands of rejections, all my queries are accepted and I'm negotiating contracts with huge sign-on bonuses…All thanks to WRITALIN." Mr. H. C.

"No one said it worked for script writers, but it does, and I've got the block buster movies to prove it!" Q.T.

Warnings

Operating heavy machinery (heavier than a keyboard) is not recommended for up to twelve hours after dosing WRITALIN. Other known side effects may include long-winded soliloquies, jumping genres, and improbable confessions.

Product testing of this drug on writers from various genres resulted in genre-specific side effects. Historical writers were found to fall into research worm holes. One poor gentleman is still there studying the effects of the ruffled shirt on sixteenth century homosexuals. Science Fiction writers report that they can't stop watching reruns of Lost In Space. A small group of poets was found to begin speaking in rhyme, or as in two cases, iambic pentameter. No antidote for these rare side effects has been found. (But then based on those few cases, why bother?)

Order yours today.
Get published tomorrow!
What's holding YOU back?

THE GAY NINETIES

An invitation to Bob's Gay Nineties party arrived in my post. Bob was the president of the local costumer's guild, Frock Tarts, which I recently joined. I was drawn to the guild because of the authenticity of their costumes as well as the fine craftsmanship each garment displayed. I knew they were notorious for their over the top parties. Rubbing elbows with other fanatic dressmakers was my goal in joining.

"Gay Nineties," I mused. How much time did I have? I responded immediately that I would be in attendance but fretted over only three weeks to turn out an outfit that would merit my membership.

Online I found scads of designs that would befit the era and several with patterns which were affordable. Before I could select the costume, I needed to find the perfect fabric. I should say fabrics as more than one was used in the dress of that day. A trip to the local fabric warehouses was in order.

Looking over the fabrics, there were many options, linen or heavy cotton for daytime, taffeta or satin for evenings and oh yes, the lace. My enthusiasm for the project plummeted when I began to estimate the cost. When you need to purchase nine yards of one fabric for the skirt alone and the price per yard was nearly twenty dollars, I would have to break the bank, so to speak. Finally, I made choices on the fabric based on cost and applicability, then the costume took form.

In all, this vintage Victorian outfit set me back over two hundred dollars, but that included the outrageous shoes I found on eBay. And a flamboyant hat.

As this was the first costume I undertook as a member of the guild, I wanted it to be perfect. Taking all the steps, I fit the dress form to my measurements and carefully cut the fabric, checking measurements along the way. The undergarments would have to be constructed as well to maintain the authenticity. Costuming required obsessive detail and flawless workmanship.

The party was scheduled for Saturday the eighth, and on the seventh, I was still hand sewing the pearls and lace trim, and the skirt needed hemming too. Working past midnight, caused me to sleep in on Saturday, leaving me only scant hours to complete my work, then steam and press. As no mention of a place to change was offered, I needed to wear the costume to the party. All the more important to get that final pressing done right. And the detail wouldn't stop there. What about hair and makeup?

Planning in advance, I located the right shade of rouge and lip gloss and swept my hair up into the style of that day. The over-the-top hat completed the ensemble which would have to be pinned on after I arrived.

Standing before the full-length mirror, I marveled at my work. In the time given I had designed and constructed a garment that would easily pass for the real thing. A dress with long poufy sleeves and high neckline, lace on the collar and cuffs, and a hat that brought out the colors of the shirred bodice and waistband. The hat was festooned with feathers. My sewing room was a mess, every scrap of fabric, thread, and pins that had fallen to the floor while I worked, were still there. The pattern pieces lay on the floor, time was too precious to stop and carefully fold the tissue back into the envelope. I shut the door leaving it all for later.

With the invitation on the console for driving instructions, I drove carefully to the far side of town for the party. Seeing an old car in passing, I thought how marvelous it would be to arrive in a horse-drawn carriage, but too late for that. Only a couple of cars were parked in the long circular driveway, and a glance at the clock told me I was early. Always awkward to be early but better to get out of the car before the skirt creased any further. I carefully climbed out and affixed the hat, doing a check in the side view mirror. I practically pranced to the front door.

"Goodness gracious me," Bob said as he opened the door. "Don't you look...well, like the bee's knees, or cat's pajamas. I can never get those straight."

My smile disappeared as I realized that Bob and the other guests were not in costume. "Did I misunderstand? The invitation said Gay Nineties..."

"Ha ha," Bob laughed. "Come in, that's funny."

"What?" asked a striking man wearing tuxedo tails and board shorts. He stopped when he saw my full attire. "Heavens, Bob, she thought you meant the 1890's."

"Didn't you?" I looked from Mr. Striking to Bob.

Bob put his arm around Mr. Striking and said, "No it was the 1990's when Jerry and I came out of the closet."

I was puzzled. What was he saying?

"You know the G-A-Y nineties," Mr. Striking spelled.

The doorbell rang and Bob opened the door to more guests wearing regular clothes. They brought nostalgic gifts from the 1990s; VHS tapes, a flip phone, and someone had a pair of roller blades.

In that moment I prayed to disappear, but Mr. Striking took my elbow and escorted me into the next room. "I'm Jerry," he said, "Follow my lead."

And he swooped me into a group of guests.

"Meet our newest member, and she's quite a costumer."

By the end of the evening, it was a draw. Those born before 1970 thought the Gay Nineties were the 1890s, and those born after, thought it was the 1990s.

OH BROTHER

The phone rang during dinner as usual. No caller id. Since I got up to look at the phone, I answered it. My husband glared across the table. He thought dinner should be sacred without interruptions. I thought of all those people who watch television while they eat. At least we sit at the table across from each other and attempt conversation.

"Hello?" I said.

"Is this Patricia Stewart?"

"It is," I said, expecting it to be a solicitor.

"This is Mr. Vance. You don't know me."

How do you answer that? I stumbled over what to say, to be polite.

"I am calling to advise you that you have a brother."

"What? What did you say?" I didn't understand.

My husband's look changed from annoyed to concerned.

"Is there a problem? Is it one of the kids?" he said.

I shook my head at him.

"I said you have a brother," the man on the phone repeated.

"A brother? I don't have a brother. I ought to know that."

"Well, this is awkward. But you do have a

brother…now."

"What are you talking about?" My voice rose an octave, whether in anger or confusion I wasn't sure.

Jack jumped up from the table and dropped his napkin. "What is it?"

"It's a man who says I have a brother," I whispered to him, the phone still to my ear.

"…the circumstances are quite strange. Were you aware that your sister was conceived in vitro?"

"Where?"

"Not a place, but your parents experienced some difficulty conceiving after your birth. Were you aware of that?"

"No. There are eighteen years between us, I just thought…" I don't know if I ever thought about it.

"There were several embryos created but only the one implanted. There's no record of what should happen with the others. Your parents…are they still alive?"

"No, dad died last year, and mom passed away when Carol was still a baby."

"That might explain it. Was there a will?"

If there's a way, there's a will, I thought. "Yes…"

"Was there any mention of the embryos?"

"No. I would have remembered that. No there was no mention."

"Unfortunately there was a mix-up and your parents' embryos were used…and now, you have a brother."

"A brother? Really, he is my brother?"

"Same genetic material as your sister…"

"How old is he? Where does he live? How did anyone figure this out?"

"He was born last month. A routine DNA test

revealed his heritage. The birth parents are filing suit against the clinic that handled the embryos. Their own embryos were lost. And..."

"Last month? Where is this?"

"He's in Georgia and they are putting him up for adoption. I thought the least we could do was inform the family members. Perhaps..."

"I'm fifty-three years old, there is no way I can take on an infant."

"What?" Jack had grown tired of hearing only my side of the conversation and returned to the table. On hearing that, he dropped his fork, knocked over his coffee cup and nearly fell out of his chair as he raced to the phone.

"Perhaps you could talk this over with your sister, she might be in a position to raise him?"

Jack took the phone from me. "Look I don't know what your scam is or why you are calling here, but we are not interested. Do not call us back." Jack ended the call and slammed the phone on the table. "You shouldn't have answered that call; it interrupted our dinner."

I sat down, trying to remember what the man's name was, and if it could be possible, or if it was just a scam like Jack assumed.

HARRIET'S WILD RIDE

Harriet is a feisty old broad. Don't know all her history but keeping her here at the home is a mighty big chore. It's not a lock down facility, nor is she a dementia patient. She moves to her own music and is known to wander off. We never know where she might be headed or when. Last week she talked of volunteering with the local fire department. Wanted to do a ride along in the fire truck. This morning she asked our driver to take her to the pharmacy. She went into the store. The driver told us he watched her enter. Then he waited.

Within minutes his attention turned toward the fire station across the street. A big red fire engine pulled out with suited-up firemen hanging onto the sides. As the vehicle entered the street, the driver recognized Harriet waving from the front of the cab. It couldn't be Harriet. But when he scouted the store looking for her, he realized it was.

Tonight at dinner, she held a captive audience telling about her escapade. Seems the firemen were willing to give an old lady a ride. She assumed it would be a brief trip around the block. She was surprised when they suited her up in overalls, boots, jacket and helmet. They helped her up into the cab and told her to put on the safety belt. When the other firefighters also suited up and climbed onto the engine, she worried that maybe they were on a call to a fire. Her thoughts of a cozy joy ride vanished. That's when the siren went off, signaling danger. As they rocketed down main street, cars pulled to the curb allowing them passage. People stared and Harriet sat tensely in her seat.

Being only a hundred and fifteen pounds but five foot nine, her body slipped and skidded on the seat with every turn. To avoid crashing into the driver or falling off the seat, she kept her feet firmly planted on the floor. She looked at the driver questioning what was happening. He gave her a stern look. His lips moved, but she couldn't hear anything other than the siren. Should have learned to lip read, she thought. When they came to a stop at a red light, the driver leaned over to her.

"Take your foot off the siren button on the floor."

"What?" She heard him but was embarrassed by her mistake. Quickly she lifted both feet and the siren was silenced. "Did I do that?"

He nodded, then chuckled. "Helluva ride, huh?"

She smiled, glad to know he wasn't going to berate her.

"Do you want us to drop you off somewhere?"

"Oh gracious me. I live at Holiday Acres. It would be a hoot to arrive in the fire engine."

All that was yesterday. We've been looking for Harriet since breakfast today. Someone said next on her bucket list was a helicopter ride. The Coast Guard station has been alerted.

INTRO TO DRAMA

It was a dark and stormy Tuesday morning when I set out for my nine o'clock class. I parked on the north side of campus, the only parking spot I could find, then trudged across the soccer field. By the time I arrived at the classroom, my shoes were wet, my socks were wet, and I was in a foul mood. Instead of being located in the new modern three-story Humanities building, this class had been relegated to the double row of portable buildings on the other side of campus. I knew from experience these classrooms were small, dingy and never warm in winter, nor cool in summer.

I opened the door to find that there were only twenty-four desks, and more than half were already filled. I quickly took a seat. In no time, it was standing room only, yet more students arrived. A few sat on the floor leaning against the wall, and many stood along the back or in between rows of desks. These crowded conditions raised the temperature, fogging the windows, and making an uncomfortable environment that much worse.

Dr. Hoover strode in, weaving his way through the throng of students. He wore a tweed jacket, shirt and tie, and carried a well-worn leather briefcase, which he set down on the desk as he surveyed the classroom. This professor had a reputation for being a stickler about details but perhaps that only applied to his job as director of student productions.

Normally, the first class sessions in college consisted of reviewing the assigned textbook(s), going over the grading process, and setting expectations. Not this one.

As the bell rang, denoting the start of class, Dr. Hoover said, "Take notes. We've got a lot of ground to cover." And he began his lecture. He spoke at a hundred-eighty words per minute, rarely pausing, starting with Greek tragedy working his way toward Shakespeare. He noted years, and names of dramas, who wrote what, and when. It was all new to me. He spouted words that I did not know neither what they meant nor how to spell them, but it did not deter me from leaving a phonetic interpretation hoping that the text would clear it up later.

I counted myself lucky. I had a seat, and my pen flew across the page laying down notes. Around me, there were less-prepared students, no note paper, no pen and then those with no seat or writing surface. As I wrote, I heard several students talking.

"This wasn't what I expected," a boy said.

"I know," a girl whispered, "I understood this was an easy A."

"No way," another commented.

Among this murmur were the sounds of pages being turned and books closing. The boy in front of me was shaking his head and searching the catalog probably seeking an alternative class. One or two students standing at the back of the room must have left because I heard the door open and close several times. No distraction caused Dr. Hoover to slow his pace.

After ninety minutes, the bell sounded and Dr. Hoover concluded, "Quiz on Thursday, read the first three chapters, but fifty percent of the test comes from class notes."

The students silently filed out of the classroom. There was a somber tone to the air like joy had been sucked out of everyone. This class was going to take a lot of effort for only two credits. But I needed those credits to satisfy the humanities requirement for graduation. I decided to stick it out.

On Thursday when I returned to the class, there were barely a dozen students. Dr. Hoover strode in looking us over.

"That's better," he said, "I like to thin out those who are not serious about drama." There was no quiz that day or any day. No tests, and he never spoke so rapidly again.

"Life's a stage," I jotted in the margin of my Intro to Drama textbook.

THE LAST TIME I SAW BILLY

At ten, after seeing *Close Encounters*, my cousin Billy announced that he was part alien. He didn't claim to have been abducted, but a descendant. Instead of shaking hands, he extended his left index finger to meet yours ala *E.T.* We cousins rolled our eyes at him behind his back.

He's an adult now but still starts every conversation at our family gatherings with news of UFOs coming to claim him.

This Thanksgiving we drew Secret Santa names among the cousins. I got Billy's name. I decided to end his ranting about being an alien by giving him a DNA test kit.

I watched when he opened it at Christmas. He didn't hesitate. He swabbed inside his cheek, sealed the swab into the plastic bag and stuffed it back into the return envelope. The instructions said it could take six to eight weeks for the results. I marked my calendar and invited everyone to Pie Day at my house on March 14.

On that morning, Aunt Kate called. She throttled me with a full rant about sticking my nose into other people's business and not knowing when to shut my trap. When she was done, I called my mom, Kate's sister, to see if she knew what was going on.

Mom told me that Kate had worked at the Star of the

Sea Catholic church on the East side. One day she found a baby boy that had been left at the church. She took him home. She intended to stop at the police station and hand him over, but something made her change her mind. She moved and started over as mother to the boy. She never disclosed to anyone that Billy was not her natural son, not even the priest in the confessional, until now.

I had no idea.

I also didn't know Billy sent away for a second DNA test using hairs from his mother's brush and a straw he placed in her iced tea. The results proved to him that he was not his mother's son and he confronted her with this. That cemented his case for alien genes.

A little while later the cousins arrived for pie. Cousin Billy came last. He'd shaved his head and had grown a mustache dyed Day-Glo green. He wore a silver spandex body suit and tried to give the Spock 'Live Long and Prosper' finger spread. When I handed him a slice of cherry pie, he laughed and said he no longer ate Earth food. He pulled a freeze-dried packet of astronaut ice-cream from inside his spandex suit. Who knew they had pockets?

Later, he said he wanted to tell me something.

"Something personal," he said.

I followed him to the front yard.

"I want to thank you for the DNA test." He pulled out his ancient flip phone, and spewed a steam of nonsense, both recognizable syllables and clicks and snaps.

I gawked at him.

He winked at me and translated, "Beam Me Up, Scotty."

I laughed.

He sparkled in the sunlight in that silver suit. I blinked at the glare. He seemed to shimmer, then he was gone. Gone. There was no one in sight. Nothing to hide behind. He was just gone.

I returned to the backyard. The cousins were all laughing about Billy and his suit and green mustache. I hesitated before saying anything.

"Well, is he gone?" Cousin Peggy asked.

What could I say? If I told them what I had witnessed, they would make as much fun of me as we made of Billy. "Yep, he's gone alright," I said.

THE LOG CABIN

When five-year-old Penny saw the color ad for the log cabin, she tore it out of the magazine and asked her mother to read it to her. She could pick out a few words, but if this was for sale, she wanted one. The photograph showed a log cabin with a front door and a window, it was child sized. There were two kids inside, a boy and a girl, and from their faces you knew they were having a great time.

Penny's mom sat down and read it. It advertised a log cabin, perfect for children's play and only ninety-nine cents. Penny clapped her hands together and ran off to get her piggy bank. She knew she had that much in it.

"I don't think that it's all you expect. Not for only ninety-nine cents," her mother said.

That same opinion was expressed by her father and her older brother. "I think they'll gyp you," he said.

Penny's enthusiasm would not be dampened. She carried the four-inch ad with her and showed it to everyone she met. "See, I'm getting this log cabin." Kids her age were envious and begged to be invited over to play in it. "We could even have sleep overs," Nickie said.

Six weeks passed and still no log cabin. Every day, Penny ran to meet the mail delivery. Each day left her disappointed until a postcard arrived. She ran to her mother, "What does it say?"

Her mother read: "We received your order, however, the thirty-seven cents for shipping and handling was not included. Please remit."

That was the first crack in her longing. "Another thirty-seven cents and still no log cabin. How long do I have to wait?" The summer was almost over and her plans for camping out in the log cabin were disappearing.

Her mother quickly addressed an envelope and taped one quarter, one dime and two pennies to an index card and mailed it off.

Another six weeks went by. Penny was now in the first grade. After school one day, Penny noticed a large manila envelope on the table. Her mother told her it was addressed to her.

"What is it?" Penny asked.

"Open it," her mother said.

Penny peeled off the back flap and peered into the envelope. A folded plastic sheet was all that was inside. Carefully she pulled it out and examined it. The thin plastic film was white with purple markings. As she opened it further, she realized that it was some sort of square. The markings were for a door and a window. "What's this?" she cried in frustration. She tried to stand the square on the ground. It was three-feet high, and easily fell flat. Over and over she tried. "It's stupid," she cried.

Mother read words printed on the plastic. "To be placed over a card table...cut along the dotted lines to open the door and window...fun for two children."

Like the air being released from a balloon, Penny deflated, realizing this flimsy plastic was her log cabin. She kicked it and went to her room. When her brother came home, and mom explained about the log cabin, he brought the card table in from the garage and set it up in the family room. It was the right size for the card table, and two small children could fit under the table and look out the door or window after it was cut along the dotted line. Then he went to get Penny.

She held the ad in one hand and compared it against the white plastic with purple lines. The color photograph showed a brown log cabin with a green wooden door and a four-paned window. Penny said, "They lied to me."

"That's advertising for you," her father said.

The log cabin sat there for nearly a week, then Penny pulled the plastic off the table, wadded it up and threw it into the garbage can.

THE MISSING SOCK

Everyone shares the experience of putting two socks into the washer, but only one coming out of the dryer. Here is a story about where one sock went.

My father worked as a young executive for the Bank of America in their San Francisco world headquarters. By day he dressed in the mandated dark suit, starched white shirt and sincere tie. At home he was a different man surrounded by his wife and seven daughters. He dressed in paint-splattered pants and frayed sweatshirts. That's how I remember my dad.

We lived in a rented hundred-year-old farmhouse in a rural community which meant he had an hour commute by train to and from work each day. Mom took care of the children and the home. She did the shopping, cooking, and laundry at least until an incident caused my father to demand that his dress shirts be professionally laundered. He prided himself on a neat and professional appearance.

One day as he walked from the office to a nearby restaurant for lunch, he noted a radio and television personality on the street. Whenever this happened, he would recreate the scene for us over dinner. That night there was a postscript to the celebrity sighting.

"You'll never guess who I saw today," he said.

"Who?" we questioned in unison.

"I'll give you a clue," he said. "They are on television."

"Hmmm, Jonathan Winters?" mother guessed.

"No," he said and took another bite of dinner. "Pass the salt."

"Walt Disney?" I guessed.

"No," he said.

"Mickey Mouse?" my sister blurted.

He shook his head at my sister which only made the next one throw out her guess.

"Donald Duck?"

"No," he said using his best Donald Duck impersonation. "He has red hair, that's two clues."

"Red Skelton?" my mother guessed.

"Forget it." He took a long drink of his iced tea and setting the glass down said, "I saw Arthur Godfrey."

"Who?" we asked in unison. Only mother recognized the name.

"You know, the morning show on television. Radio too."

This was met with a chorus of "oh." We didn't know who he meant.

"Here's the thing," he said. "I saw him approaching on Market Street, and I wanted to say something. Say how we watched his program. I straightened up, pulled down the sleeves of my jacket so that I would give the right impression. I noticed then that my left shirt sleeve was longer than the right. I thought it odd, so tugged on the right sleeve but it was already extended. Why was the left sleeve longer? I pulled on it and to my surprise, it continued to lengthen. Tugging more, it revealed that it was not my sleeve at all but one of the girls anklets. I quickly wadded it up and tucked it into my pocket. When I looked up, Mr. Godfrey had already passed by."

I remember thinking it funny, but his tone warned me that was the wrong response. What he felt was shame, embarrassment. That's when he told my mother that from now on his shirts would go to the commercial laundry.

Of course, that led to a whole new misadventure when another man with the same name used the same cleaner. Mom picked up what she thought were dad's shirts only to find that they gave her the wrong ones. It worked out, but now we knew there was more than one Paul Hansen in town.

And that led to our telephone screening skills. We girls answered the one phone at home when it rang. If they asked for dad, we were to first question which Paul Hansen they meant. He was not the brick layer nor the insurance salesman. We became good at screening his calls without having to tell them he was the banker.

My father instructed us to be courteous on the phone. Though he wasn't always. Because he had to rise early to catch the commuter train, our bedtime was nine o'clock and that meant no phone calls after nine. One night a girl called to talk to my sister. By then they were in high school.

She politely asked, "Mr. Hansen, may I please speak to Steffi?"

"Hell no," he said and hung up.

* * *

Years later I heard an interview on the radio where Mr. Godfrey talked about how people were always auditioning in front of him, as if he would invite anyone from the street to be on his show. "Once," he said, "I saw a well-dressed businessman who as he passed by, pulled something from his sleeve as if by magic. I turned back to see what it was, but the man continued on without addressing me."

I laughed. Could that have been my dad?

NINE TO FIVE

She rolls over, feels the sun blinking through the fluttering curtains. The morning air wafts gently. She sighs, looks at the clock. Then hefts herself from under the down comforter and hangs her legs over the edge of the bed. Wiggling her toes, she waits for the tingling to stop. She stands and stretches.

Under the luxurious stream of water, she is thankful for the illegal showerhead. The water completely envelops her. She closes her eyes and remembers a tropical waterfall, a long time ago. He was there with her that day. They played in the water then withdrew behind the falls.

The phone on the bathroom counter rings. Rather it plays the tune from "Nine to Five" signaling that it's her boss. She must answer it. She turns off the water and reaches for the phone. She has done this many times before. Answered professionally just as if she was sitting behind a desk. She can do it one more time. She thinks, *I'll quit today. Well, not today, but soon. No more of this being tethered to the phone, to this person. To their demands.*

This time her reach across the span between the shower and the counter is different. Maybe the phone is a few too many centimeters to the left, or she is not standing as near the shower door as usual. The reach is too far and her center of gravity wrong. She slips and falls onto the tile floor. Thud. The phone is not totally out of her reach, her finger touches it, sends it spinning, and it too falls to the floor. Splat. As she goes down knowing there is no way to recover and that the phone is also falling, she hears the ring one more time. She knows her boss is cursing her for not being available. She wonders about the gravity experiments where you drop two objects at the same time and the teacher asks which will land first. What is the basis of that? Distance? Weight? Mass? Splat.

All this goes through her mind in that split second of time as she tumbles. Her feet still in the shower, her ankle broken in the fall on the four-inch lip of stone. Her left hip hits the floor first, then her cheek, her nose. Her left shoulder dislocates and her arm lays at an unnatural angle to her body. The phone does not fare much better. The glass face splinters into a spider web of fractures. Her right arm outstretches as if in a last attempt to break the fall of the phone.

All is quiet. Then the beep of voice mail.

NAN'S MUSE

All the way through undergrad school, Nan wrote. She worked on the college newspaper and wrote news stories, gossip columns, editorials and every once in a while, did sports page coverage. In between assignments, she started countless novels, short stories, and poetry, but nothing was ever good enough. Not good enough by her standards to submit for publication. Then came graduate school and Nan worked towards a Masters in Fine Arts.

"Whatever made me think I could hope to succeed in this," she asked herself over and over again. More frequently when she had a writing assignment due, she thought about quitting. Her parents offered encouragement. "Don't underestimate yourself, you've always been good with words," her mother said. "And storytelling," her father added.

Just before graduation, she stepped into a crosswalk and was plowed down by a speeding car. She bounced off the hood of the car and landed in the road, then got nicked by another vehicle before passersby blocked traffic waiting for the ambulance. It was three weeks in the hospital and several surgeries later before she was released to in-home care.

She had to leave school. It also meant that the

healing process, which involved physical therapy and a lot of pain relievers, kept her in a perpetual fog.

One morning she sat down at her keyboard and began writing. Truth was she awoke in the midst of typing and seeing that she was at mid-story, swallowed her misgivings and just kept typing. Under the influence of the pain pills she became insatiable. She would type out thousands of words per day and edit them with little deletion. She questioned how good it really was since she realized this was not her sane self, but she chose not to question the gift as she came to think of it.

After three months, she was walking unaided, and her physical therapist suggested she get back into school to finish her degree. To her surprise, her advisor offered that if she submitted a completed work of sixty thousand words, they would accept that, and grant graduation. If it merited at least a B.

Nan weighed her options. If she submitted this work and it was accepted, she was done. Otherwise, she would have to move back to be near the campus, find an apartment, get registered, go to classes and complete an additional fifteen units of work. The offer was tempting.

Going through her class notes, she found a reputable copy editor and made arrangements for them to review her work and provide comments. If they didn't tear it to shreds, she would do the edit and submit it. She had thirty days in which to act. The copy editor accepted the manuscript and agreed to turn it in ten days, Nan was elated. But after five days, she received a call and an offer for publication.

"What? There must be some mistake."

"Why?"

"I submitted this for editing, not publication."

"I realize that. But this is good. Real good. I work for Penguin and I know they are looking for material like this. Especially from new young authors. I can almost guarantee you that they will sign you."

"But I need to edit and submit for my masters…"

"No worries. You can do both. I'll send it back with my edit suggestions along with a submittal form and a contract for representation. You get your schoolwork done and then we will publish your first novel."

Nan set down the phone and pinched herself. She looked at her prescription bottle, only three pills left. She was only to take them when in pain now, not every four hours as she had been. Was her work really that good? Could she complete the novel without them?

The next twenty days flew by. The copy editor's notes were not. No major rewrite. A little more description here, a little less there. Fix the grammar and spelling errors. Nan submitted the seventy-two-thousand-word novel to her advisor ten days ahead of the due date. Then she waited for the grade.

Two days later she got a call. "Nan, that was your best work. I think you have a publishable novel…" Nan listened as the advisor droned on about her friend who used to be an agent but might have some contacts and other helpful ideas.

"But my grade?" Nan interjected.

"Oh, heavens, you got an A."

Nan sat silent. "An A," she whispered to herself. "Maybe I can do this."

Nan's novel was published and on bookshelves for the holiday season. The next eighteen months were a whirlwind of book signings and on-air interviews. Nan had never experienced the limelight and warmed up to it after the first six months. Her agent pulled her back into the atmosphere when she said, "So, how is the second book coming along? The publisher will be looking to get it out as soon as possible."

"I hadn't thought of that," Nan said, but what she wanted to say was that she had no idea what to do about the second book, or the third. That old nagging feeling that she didn't have it in her was taking hold.

"Well send me what you have, maybe I can help."

"No. Not yet," Nan stuttered, "but soon."

She looked over her schedule and saw that she had a two-week break coming up with no interviews, no signings. That is what she needed – a break from all the running around. Then she could sit down and start on that novel.

The break came and went with nothing to distract her, but her own insecurity. The next two days she ignored calls from her agent, then turned the phone off. Packing for the coming road trip, she found the prescription bottle with the final three pain pills. She took one and two hours later, another. That evening she sat down and pounded out eight thousand words. She had the plot for a trilogy set up, and jotted notes about how the story would be split between the three novels. It was five o'clock in the morning and the sun was streaking across the horizon. She had a plane to catch, emailed the draft and notes to her copy editor, then headed to the airport. She kept the phone off and stuck to her schedule. She avoided any thoughts about new deadlines or failure. Instead she basked in her own popularity and prayed fervently for another shot at success.

She worried that the first novel was written while she was zoned-out on pain meds and the fact that the only viable copy she was able to produce afterwards was also under the same influence. Panicking, she called her doctor and lied that a recent fall was making her leg hurt again and could they renew her prescription. She would have to fill it while on the road but would make an appointment to be examined as soon as she returned. No problem, they gave her another sixty-day supply.

She took two tablets after dinner and was headed to bed, but first a soak in the tub. That's when the idea popped into her head and she grabbed her laptop and started typing. She moved from the tub to the desk and rapidly turned her thoughts into words on the page. As quickly as the idea materialized her fingers took over and there was a part of her that looked at what she was doing, and marveled. But back to work, she scolded herself. This creativity doesn't happen without a little help.

She left the hotel room only when she had an appointment. Luckily they were staying in Manhattan for five days and there were nine appointments, but most tended to be in early evening, so she typed upon her return till noon, then ate, slept and started over again. By the end of the two weeks on the road, she had finished two of the three books in the new trilogy. She didn't tell anyone what she was doing, she needed to get ahead of the demands. She needed to figure it out.

Still strung out on the meds, she listened as the PR person introduced her. How many times had she heard this? Had she ever listened to the words? She wanted to vomit. This was not who she was or how she thought of herself. When had she become this person? She took her seat and looked at her audience. A hundred chairs had been set in this upscale bookstore, but not more than twenty were filled. At the same time, people shopped in the aisles behind them, kids ran around, a puppet show was in process in the far corner, and the ever-present and pervasive espresso machine grinding, whirring and spritzing. She heaved a sign and opened the book. They always had her read the same passage. She started to read. The words were slightly out of focus. She shook the book, wiped her eyes and scrutinized the lighting. Then began again.

Most of the time she read, she was amazed at the writing, the story. She had no knowledge of writing the book. It seemed to leap from her. What Nan dreaded most about the readings were the Q&A after. They asked how she had come up the characters, the setting, the plot. She had no idea and lacked the imagination to dream up a plausible story for them. Instead the hemmed and hawed and the PR person tried to field as many questions as possible saying that the author was an introvert – very shy – and tired from her busy schedule.

Either way, they bought the books and wondered how this mousy little woman could have given them such a suspenseful block buster. And Nan wondered too.

On Bended Knee

Maxine surveyed the lunch tables at the Happy Acres Retirement Home. She chose a seat next to a well-dressed gentleman. He introduced himself as Willy. Maxine noticed his startling blue eyes, easy smile, and naked ring finger on his left hand. And he was very handsome.

Maxine regretted dressing in her jeans and sweatshirt. A sweatshirt with holes in the elbows and a big orange jack-o-lantern on the front. She chose it to match the autumn weather, but now wished that she was better dressed. She would like to get to know Willy and felt making a positive impression was the way to do it.

Over lunch they talked about their hobbies. She learned that he too loved gardening. She mentioned that she had trees that needed pruning; he offered to help saying he had a lot of experience, but no tools.

"I've got the tools," she said.

Maxine had a weak heart for good looking men. She easily fell in love with such men and had been married seven times, each time to a man more handsome than the last. At seventy-seven, she didn't hold out hope for a number eight. Harry died the year before, and she decided this would be her last year in the house. The yard work was more than she could handle, and the house was too big. She was touring the senior residence when they invited her to join them for lunch. Then she met Willy. The fact that he was already a resident was another advantage to making the move now.

Willy arrived as scheduled to help her with the pruning. He wore pressed blue jeans and a plaid Pendleton. Maxine was dressed in new slacks and a sweater set, much too nice for gardening, but not too nice for Willy.

He took the pruners and climbed the ladder.

"You certainly make it look easy," she said watching him thin the branches.

When he climbed down the ladder, he said, "It's rather warm for an autumn day." He unbuttoned and removed the Pendleton shirt. Underneath he wore a Hard Rock Café t-shirt. Maxine admired his lean torso but when his forearms were exposed, she looked away in shock.

"Oh my," she said. Maxine had never seen a tattoo before.

Willy laughed looking down at his arms. "Twenty-two years in the Navy. I've got a lot of ink."

"Ink?" Maxine repeated, feeling dizzy.

Willy dropped the pruners, and proudly lifted his t-shirt to reveal the battleship scene on his chest.

"Yes, you certainly have a lot of ink," she said, fanning herself with her hand.

"Do you like it?" he asked.

"Well, it's colorful, and it seems to be well drawn."

"Only the best," he said bending down on one knee.

Maxine gasped. She thought he was going to propose. That was how her husbands had done it, down on one knee. But she and Willy hardly knew each other. She took a step back, wiped her sweaty palms on her pants, and wondered if she should say yes.

Willy, down on one knee, looked up at Maxine, a playful glint in his eyes.

Maxine took a deep breath. She knew she didn't have too many years left, why not spend them with this handsome man.

Still kneeling, Willy lifted his left pant leg to show her the tattoo of his childhood pet, a German Shepherd named Lucky.

Maxine choked back a giggle, thinking he was going to propose. How preposterous. Then she fainted.

MY GOOSE WAS COOKED

Thanksgiving Day dawned bright—so bright that I wondered why and opened the blinds. "Snow," I breathed. "Not today." There was a good ten inches sitting atop the fence rails, and it was still coming down. It's not that I don't like an occasional snowfall, but my Aunt Mary and Uncle Carl were coming. Mary had said not to worry, she'd bring the bird. What if they couldn't get down off the mountain? I hadn't bought a turkey. In fact, the only meat I had was six hot dogs. I thought this could be the worst Thanksgiving ever.

Around ten, I called, just to be sure Aunt Mary was on her way. The phone rang and rang. Now I had to toss a coin. Did it mean that they were on their way, or that the phone service was out? I still had time to run to the store and buy a small turkey and get it in the oven. It'd mean we'd eat later than four, but we'd eat.

At eleven, my sister, her husband and five kids arrived. "Smells good," she said. "Where's the turkey?"

I explained the dilemma to her.

"Let's go to the store," she said.

At the store, there were only five turkeys left. I purchased the smallest one, a frozen chunk weighing twenty-three pounds.

Denise filled the bathtub with hot water and floated the turkey. "We'll just keep the water hot," she said. I saw her husband Bill shrug his shoulders.

"You should have let me deep fry it, he said as he hunkered down in front of the television.

At two, the doorbell rang and there stood Aunt Mary and Uncle Carl. I threw my arms around them. "So glad to see you," I said noticing that Mary had a small canvas sack in her hand. "Can I help you with the turkey?" I asked hoping it was still in the truck.

"Turkey?" she said.

My stomach clenched. My mind jumped between the six hot dogs in the refrigerator and the twenty-three-pound turkey-berg floating in the bathtub. My plans for the perfect Thanksgiving dinner were falling apart.

She read the panic on my face and laughed. "I never said turkey. I said I'd bring the bird."

Bird, turkey – what was the difference? I thought.

"Carl butchered a goose this morning." She lifted the bag and held it out to me. A downy feather floated through the air.

"Oh…" I took a deep breath; everything would be fine.

"Let's get it in the oven," she said, and I followed her into the kitchen.

She dumped the bird into the sink, rinsed it, then plopped it into the roasting pan.

That skinny little goose barely covered the rack. How would it be enough for six adults and five growing children?

She salted it and plunged it into the oven. "Set it for four hundred degrees," she said. "It should be done in, oh, forty-five minutes."

"Really?" If that was so, I had to get the potatoes mashed, bake the dressing, make the salad.

"What about gravy?" I asked.

"Whatever you got," she said.

She joined Carl and Bill in front of the television. The kids were in the den with their computer games, and I rushed through the steps. Thanksgiving dinner was coming together. That is, until the smoke alarm sounded. Smoke billowed out when I opened the oven door. The roasting pan was full of grease. I yelled for Aunt Mary.

As she entered the room, the grease caught fire, and flames leapt up. I slammed the oven door shut, spilling the flaming liquid. There was a full roaring fire inside my oven. We both screamed. That brought the men in.

"Fricassee," Carl said.

"More like barbeque," Bill said.

"Flambé," said Denise.

Bill was ever ready with the fire extinguisher and aimed it at the oven, then opened the door and swoosh.

"Blackened," I said looking at the what was left of the charred bird.

Moments later, Carl shouted from the bathroom, "What's this?"

That's when I remembered the turkey. The bird was thawing out. Bill said, "I've been wanting to deep fry one of these babies in oil."

Denise rolled her eyes.

Bill jogged outside and was back with a box clearly marked. It was a turkey fryer. "You got propane?" he asked.

Bill and his deep fat fryer saved Thanksgiving that year. Every year since we leave the cooking of the bird to him. But it is cooked outside, away from the house, and I have a nice pre-cooked turkey breast in the refrigerator, just in case.

THE RETURNS DEPARTMENT

Having worked in customer service, I read the ad with interest. "Wanted: Experienced Customer Service Clerk to work with special gift returns. Work from home. Top dollar paid. Post resume to …."

It was exactly what I wanted. I had three kids at home, a husband who drank his paycheck, and a landlord who showed up to collect rent on the first of every month. I needed income, steady work without more expenses. I sent off my resume without a further thought and kept my ear tuned to the sound of email for the following day. Just before midnight I got the response, scheduling me for a skype interview the following day.

When the call came in, the interviewer was not what I expected. He was twenty-ish, wore a full beard and shoulder-length hair. It looked like he was dressed in a robe. He explained that he worked for a purveyor who provided custom gifts and sometimes complications arose where the bearer wanted to return the gift. There was no monetary transaction, so each return had to be arranged differently. They were looking to hire someone to ask the right questions, assess any damage, and quickly make a decision about the best response. Following the face-to-face interview with the gifted person, the customer service provider (me) would fill out a report and advise the outcome to headquarters.

I nodded during the entire conversation. This was exactly up my alley.

"Any questions?" he asked.

"What days of the week would I work and are there specific hours?"

"You can work any time you like, but we require a minimum of twenty hours per week. You will log into our site and respond to the messages. Your time on the site will validate the number of hours worked. You can skype through the site with our clients to satisfy their requests."

"What is the pay?"

"Typically, an experienced agent can make $5,000 per month but many will opt to take one of the returned gifts in lieu of pay for that month. Only one gift can be regifted to yourself during any thirty-day period."

"The, uh, gifts are that valuable?" This was sounding better and better.

"When they are requested, the clients usually specify them as priceless."

"I accept. When do I start?" It sounded too good to be true.

"You will receive an email shortly with your login and a temporary password. Login within the next twenty-four hours and reset the password. Then you can start work with any client. We do prefer that you start with the oldest message and work to the newer ones."

"Is there a minimum number of clients that I should work with per day?"

"Start with one, some take more time than others.

Welcome aboard. I guess I should warn you that some of the issues go back quite a way. Good luck."

After terminating the call, I had a lot more questions. Where is the headquarters? What is the name of the company? What type of gifts? But I assumed that once I logged in and started, this would become apparent to me.

The login routine was easy. I was prompted to select an avatar. I was to create my online persona, one who looked real enough to spook me. It started with ethnicity, gender, age, height, weight, hair color, hair style, eye color, facial tics and on and on. Was it better to pick something like me or unlike me? Would they hear my voice, or would my voice be modulated to match my avatar? So many questions. No wonder they just wanted you to make one call per day. I chose a Scandinavian female named Astrid. She had long straight blonde hair, blue eyes, was five feet ten inches tall, and weighed one hundred twenty pounds. I was short, overweight after three kids, and dark-haired, about as far from Astrid as an asteroid.

The screen read, "scanning" and the camera snapped my picture.

I waited for the next instruction. Would it say "wrong" or "error" because I should have selected an avatar more like myself?

The screen read, "Good morning, Astrid, here is your customer service request."

I clicked the digital envelope and the message opened. Instead of an email written by a client it was an actual video of a person explaining why the requested gift was unacceptable and must be returned.

The image was of a man standing in waist-high water. Behind him, people were screaming and dogs barking. Rain fell in torrents. His language was unknown to me and I looked into the toolbar for a translation button. Immediately his text was translated into a running subtitle under the image.

"Stop the rains. I know we asked for the rain, but it has been going on for forty days and forty nights, and people are drowning. Please stop the rain."

THE ROCKIN J

Dirk Weadle excelled at sneakiness. If there was a way to circumvent the law, he took it. No one knew when he made that U-turn on moral ground, but he was headed to no good. That's what Sheriff Upton said when he released him from jail.

"Three days hardly pays for his crime," the deputy said. "His lawyer got him off on a technicality."

When the sheriff handed Dirk his meager belongings, he suggested Dirk move along and leave Sunset Hills.

Dirk scoffed at him. Across town, he stopped at the café where Lucy worked. He wouldn't mind spending the night with her. He ordered the special dinner plate. As he was served, he asked about Lucy.

"She's long gone, son," the old man behind the counter said.

"Long gone? I saw her last week."

"Couldn't have been last week. She left more than two weeks ago. Headed to California."

"California?" Dirk wondered if he ought to follow her. He'd always wanted to see California.

He pulled out his wallet and showed the old man he had no bills. "Is there an ATM anywhere close by?"

"We take plastic," the old man said.

"Well, you see, they've cut me off," Dirk shrugged.

"How you gonna pay for that supper then?" the old man scratched his chin and looked Dirk up and down. From his too-long hair to his ripped jeans, Dirk did not resemble a responsible person. He pointed to the full sink of dishes. "That ought to square things up."

Dirk laughed. "No freaking way am I gonna wash your freaking dishes old man. I'll be back with the money later." He didn't wait for agreement but turned sharply and left.

"Hah! You'll never see that one again." The woman sitting at the counter said.

"You think?" The old man wiped down the counter and carried Dirk's dishes to the kitchen.

Dirk laughed. He'd pulled off another fast one. Dinner on the house. But he needed some cash in his pocket if he was driving to California. As he passed the Rocking J bar he worked out a plan.

Back in his rented room, he packed up his belongings and took the flat screen TV off the wall. He loaded up his truck after midnight, and headed back to the Rocking J. His friend Ray was behind the bar and nodded to Dirk as he came in. Dirk ordered a beer and surveyed the pool tables. Luck was with him tonight. He worked his way into a game with three young bucks. He shot the eight ball into the side pocket. In feigned embarrassment he said, "That was stupid."

In their mirth, they offered him another chance. "Double or nothing," the young scruffs said. Dirk calculated that would bring him fifty dollars.

Dirk reluctantly agreed, "Well I guess I could try."

They let him break. He deftly cleared the table and

picked up the fifty dollars.

The boys realized they'd been hustled and tried to get Dirk to shoot another game.

Ray announced, "Last call," and gave Dirk his tab. Dirk roped Ray into a conversation. Asked about Lucy and did he know where she went in California. Told him about the three days he spent in jail. Asked Ray after his family.

"Nice catching up with you, Dirk, but I gotta close up."

Dirk looked around. It was just him and Ray. The Rockin J was empty.

He followed Ray to the cash register. "Hate to do this to you buddy, but I need the cash. All of it."

Ray turned. "Are you kidding?" He saw the contour of the gun in Dirk's pocket. "Okay, okay."

Dirk pocketed the wad of bills Ray took from the register. "And the ones under there." He nudged Ray with the muzzle of the gun.

Ray lifted the divider and scooped up the twenties and the one-hundred-dollar bill, handing them to Dirk.

"Thanks. You'll never see me again. I'd regret having to hurt you. Give me ten minutes before you call the cops."

Then he backed across the room, keeping his aim on Ray. He opened the door, turned toward where he left his truck, and ran.

Only his truck was gone, and in its place was a pool cue. Before Dirk could make sense of it, sirens wailed.

GRANDPA BILL

My Grandpa Bill was a character. After he retired, he played twenty-seven holes of golf every day. One time he shot a hole in one. He lived in Nebraska, and when snow fell on the golf course, he loaded Grandma into their Ford Galaxy and drove to our home in California. He played golf there until one of his buddies called and said that the courses back home were clear.

Grandma said if Grandpa would be reincarnated as a parrot, he would be more companionship to her. I wondered what that parrot would say to Grandma so that she would know it was Grandpa.

At dinner one night Grandpa said that the snow was gone in Nebraska. He and Grandma were leaving the next day. They'd been with us for almost four months. That night I kissed Grandpa goodnight, and I let Grandma hug and kiss me. I enjoyed her visits because she liked to take us on excursions that our parents weren't interested in. When the roof caved in on the local bowling alley, she took us to get a good look. You couldn't see much, but we got the chance to be there. She was up for amusement parks and for roller skating. She liked to sew and taught me how to put in a dart that wouldn't pucker, and hem my skirts so they were above the knee.

They left after breakfast and said they'd be home in three days. On the second day, my Dad ran his finger across the map and said they were probably in Colorado or Wyoming. I stared at the distance between where we lived and his finger. I wondered what they saw as they drove. My mind raced through photographs I'd seen in National Geographic.

In the middle of the night when the house was quiet with sleep, the phone on the nightstand in my parent's room rang. My father said "hello" half asleep. There were "yeses" and questions, then the lights came on. My parents got up and talked. My sister and I lay in our beds listening, trying to figure out what was going on. The phone never rang after nine; we recognized this as important. When our bedroom filled with sunlight, we crept downstairs to learn that there had been a car accident and Grandma was dead. We were kept home from school that day while mom and dad made phone calls and funeral arrangements. I sat in my room with a memory of my Grandmother that last night; the memory of the adventures we had gone on and the sewing lessons. I thought of all the funny things she had told me, like Grandpa being reincarnated as a parrot.

I went to the garage and opened my father's golf bag. He played with his dad on weekends, but he did not play twenty-seven holes of golf every day like Grandpa. I unzipped the side pocket where the golf balls were kept, pulled them out one by one, inspecting each, and holding it up to my ear. Once, when Grandma said that Grandpa liked golf more than her, she had leaned over and whispered in my ear that if she could come back as a golf ball, he would pay more attention to her.

A Dog Called Spite

My wife and I agreed that now was a good time to bring a dog into the family. Saturday in the parking lot of a local store there was a pet adoption event. Our six-year-old son, Wyatt, went to investigate the dogs. We looked into all the pens of dogs ready and waiting to be rehomed. Wyatt couldn't tell me what sort of dog he wanted, but he knelt and let one lick his fingers through the cage while an attendant stood watch. A dog at the end of the aisle caught my eye. He was a rascally old bulldog, and I recalled one like him from my boyhood.

There was no way this was the same dog. But I leaned in close and whispered, "Spite." His ears perked up a bit and with a great deal of labor, he pulled himself up and lolled over to me.

The attendant came to my side. "I don't … think this one would be a good … companion for your son," she said. "He's old and has a bad case of arthritis."

"How old is he?" I asked. She gave me a funny look. She was probably wondering why I would want this dog.

"We don't know his history, but we are guessing more than twelve."

I'm thirty-two and remembered Spite from the time I started school, so there was not much chance this was the same dog.

"I patted him on the head and gave him a "good

boy," then turned to see who Wyatt was talking to. More than talking, Wyatt had climbed into the pen. He was sitting inside with a sweet little terrier pup who seemed to want the boy as much as the boy wanted the dog.

I looked to the attendant.

"Better choice," she said.

After we got everyone settled at home, I told my wife about the bulldog.

"Spite? You mean Spike, right?"

"No, his name was Spite."

"That's a strange name for a dog. I've heard of Spike and it seems it would fit a Bulldog."

Now I had to rethink it. She was right. Spike would have been a great name for the dog. He was solid and square, and scary looking, but a sweetheart. I could hear my mother's voice from back then. "Spite get off the couch, Spite outside, outside." No, it was Spite, not Spike.

No matter how I pushed it from my mind, I kept going back over those memories looking for some clue. Something was missing from the picture. My mother had died when I was in high school and my close friend's family took me in for a couple of years. Spite wasn't around then. I had no memory of what happened to him.

Wyatt got to name his dog. He tried all sorts of names for a couple of days then he named him Fetch. Seemed someone had taught the dog to play ball, and not only was he good at catching the ball or the frisbee in midair, he'd trot back and lay it at your feet, then back up a foot, ready to go again. I was helping Wyatt throw the frisbee when another memory snuck in. As a young boy I was in a yard with a man. He was showing me how to throw the ball to Spite. Spite caught on even though he was only a puppy. That presented two problems. I had no other memory of Spite being small, and who was this man?

I let Wyatt play and sat down in the shade. For as long as I could remember, it had been my mother and me and Spite. And Spite was an adult, full sized. My memory went back before I started school and it was just the three of us from then on. I knew nothing of my father. When I'd ask, my mother said he was gone and not coming back. Nothing more. For some reason I worked out that he had died in Vietnam. I had nothing concrete to base that on, but it made sense to me. Maybe it matched the history of a friend's dad, or maybe I got the idea from a movie, nevertheless that is what I told anyone who asked from that point on.

My mother had no relatives and she never dated. So who was that man? I remembered him with fondness like it was a good day, but it was only a glimpse.

Online, I read about genealogy and wondered if I looked up information on my mother what I would find. It led me to a brick wall, nothing more than what I knew. I had only a few things of hers. What does a boy know about keeping family heirlooms or important papers? But I had to have something. Up in the attic storage, I found a box of stuff from back then. In it was my letterman's jacket, a yearbook, and deep in the box, a Bible. I didn't actually remember the Bible. Was it my mother's? Would Mrs. Jackson, who took me in after my mother died, have saved this for me as well?

It was a large tome, well-worn. I opened it, and it

came as a surprise to me to see foreign names I did not know listed on the front page. It showed a family tree ending with a boy who was born about the same time as me, but with a different name and birthdate. His mother's name was not my mother's name but there was a father listed. Why did my mother have this Bible? Was it even hers? How did I get it?

Online, I typed in the name of the boy and was surprised when the search brought up pages of information. He had been abducted at the age of three and never found. Also taken with the boy was his dog, Spike. His parents still posted information including enhanced photographs of what he might look like today.

He looked like me.

STOLEN WORDS

File it under the category of you-don't-know-what-you-have-until-it's-gone. Five years before, I drove across the country to study writing under her guidance. I'd applied but never received confirmation or notice of unsuitability. I didn't send the money either. But, I quit my job, paid my roommate in advance for the next month and put everything I had on coming back equipped to be a best-selling author.

That was five years ago. When they blocked me at the door because I wasn't on the list, I went around the back and in through the window. I sat quietly at the back of the room and ate up every word she spoke. Her presentation ended all too soon. As the devotees gathered around her, I saw the administrators eyeing me. I skirted the crowd and went out the way I came in.

That afternoon I hung around the hotel hoping to see her. She was the best-selling and most sought-after author. I'd read all of her books. Every one. And several more than once. She had a way with words that went beyond writing. She captured the essence of her characters, of the surroundings, the undercurrents, too. She strung her words together like priceless pearls. Often I lifted my voice and read out loud to hear the exquisiteness of her language.

It was her words. She manipulated the story with the words she plucked from her lexicon. She used more words than any other author I'd read. I sat with a dictionary to look up words that confounded me. Often she chose a word for its alternative meaning or use – but it all worked. It always worked.

Camping out in the lobby proved successful. When she entered, I overheard her tell someone she was going to relax by the pool. I went back to my car for one of her books, then tagged along with other hotel guests into the pool area through the security gate. I found a corner with three empty chaise lounges, and took the center one, throwing my towel on another. I laid back with the book open on my chest.

Like a bee to pollen, she came to me.

"Is this lounge free?" she asked.

"Yes," I said, looking over the frame of my sunglasses at her.

She smiled and nodded toward the book.

I waited until she was settled. "I was hoping to ask for an autograph…"

"Sure, but I don't have a pen."

"I do." Sitting up I offered her the book and the pen. "I was at your presentation this morning."

"Oh, did you find it useful?"

"Useful? Are you kidding me? I drove across the country to be here. You are by far my favorite author, and I would so love to learn how to write like you…"

We talked all afternoon. When the sun became too intense by the pool, we moved in and sat on her patio. She ordered iced tea for us, then we switched to

Margarita's with chips and guacamole. Afterwards, we walked to a sushi restaurant and ate our fill. All the time talking. Talking about writing.

"Words hold the magic to your writing," she said.

"Yours do."

* * *

That was then. Now I am driving across the miles again. A bond developed between us. *Why me?* I asked myself, then counted my blessings that it was me. She shared her ideas with me. Read my writing and offered guidance. More than once she responded to my cry for help. She never wrote a line in any of my novels, she never suggested a word where I could have used another. Instead, she asked me questions about my story, about my characters. She asked the what-if questions, or why-not scenarios. Now, it was my turn to help her.

A month ago, she suffered a stroke. The doctors said it was a minor one, that she should be able to recover fully. Only that's not what happened. Her health returned; the muscles that did not move on her left side awoke and were in balance with those on her right side. She could stand, sit, dance, and even drive. But the words, her words, all the words were gone.

Emails she responded to were splattered with nonsense. Phone calls were answered, but other than a mumble now and again, she was mute. Her mind seemed sharp, and she recognized the nonsense that spilled from her mouth. Her fingers typed but her brain no longer knew how to access the lexicon. We attempted to work out a code language. She liked to repeat the word chicken, so I tried to get her to use it as a positive response. "Are you feeling well today? Say chicken for yes, bull for no."

"Duck," she said.

Most assuredly that was not positive. Unable to communicate by phone or email with her, I planned to spend a month with her, hopeful that we could span this loss of language. Find another means of communication. I also wanted to see if there were other options. Options that her family and doctors had not explored. It was unconscionable to me that she would live out her life in this non-communicative existence.

The family embraced me warmly and ushered me into her study offering me the somewhat leaky airbed. She had an around the clock caregiver who looked after her. Our first day was spent in pleasant smiles but no communication. She seemed standoffish, and I was saddened further to lose her friendship. She retired early that night, and I decided to work on my latest novel. While sitting at her desk, my mind wandered. I found myself idly looking at a pile of manila folders on her desk. The first contained notes on a novel she was working on, the next one a novel recently finished. I remembered her telling me how excited her agent was to read it. Beneath it were another dozen files of manuscripts started but not completed. One stood out to me. I pulled the folder and began to scan the pages.

During the years of our friendship, she seemed generous to me. Offering to read my work, introducing me to her agent, suggesting publications I should submit to. But none of my work had been published. Her agent was pleasant enough but passed on my manuscripts. I was tired of trying and tired of working at dead-end jobs because one day I would be published. Maybe it was time to accept the fact that at thirty-one, I was never going to be a best-selling author.

Then I recognized the story I was reading. Reading more, it was one of the stories I had sent her. Many of the pages seemed to be word for word from my manuscript. What had she told me? It's too cliché? I needed to do more research? But here it was, and it was finished, but it wasn't her name. It was the name of that new fiction writer, the one that never took an interview. What the hell!

I couldn't believe it. This was insane. Anger pulsed through me, tears stung my eyes. How could she have done this to me? I thought we were friends. I wiped the tears, and paced the room thinking over what I should do. I needed to find how far this deceit went. I locked the door and dug into her filing cabinet.

One by one I pulled the other files and found that several of the stories I had sent to her were now in the name of this other author. Then a letter from her agent tied this author back to her. They were using my work. How could I have been duped? Tears dropped onto the pages. I turned on her computer and searched for the most recent work. And copied it all to my thumb drive. Then I deleted all those files from her computer. I copied all the correspondence with the agent about the already published works of mine. Then I searched the internet for a top-notch copyright attorney.

At sunrise, I packed my suitcase into my car and left before anyone noticed. There were no words to convey my feelings. I had been deceived by someone I trusted, swindled from my chance at fame. Bamboozled.

Six months later, I heard that she was still stuck wordless. Under threat, her agent switched the pen name to me and has three more of my novels in the works. One is a current best-seller. The success I longed for is bittersweet, though the royalties from the past novels as well as the interviews and book signings will help ease the pain I'm sure.

Teaching ESL

Moving from teaching English to English as a second language seemed like a piece of cake. And three years of teaching in Central America certainly qualified me. I responded to the ad "ESL instructor for illegal aliens." I was intimidated by the reference, but the pay was what I needed.

On my first day, I was ushered into a sterile room no larger than a cubicle. It had a built-in desk and a computer screen. The administrator indicated the keyboard and pointed out the microphone.

"Where are my students?" I asked looking around.

"They'll be right there," he pointed to the monitor.

"Online? You never said..."

"Not to worry," the administrator told me, "Every instructor has a translation device. It works both ways, you can hear and understand your students; and when you speak, it translates to them. Get ready, class starts now," he said, checking his watch. Abruptly he left shutting the door behind him.

The room was small, dark, and eerily quiet. I would not have taken the job if I knew it was online. I like the one-on-one interaction with my students.

A bell sounded, and the screen came to life. One by one students logged into the session. No pictures, only dialog boxes. There were two boxes blinking. One said, "Address All" the other, "Address One." I clicked the first and began the lesson. The screen showed that I was to open with "Good Morning." But in times of stress my Texas drawl kicks in and I said, "Good morning y'all."

Each of the dialog boxes showed a response. I clicked on them one by one, and each played a somewhat mechanical voice responding, "Good morning." The messages seemed slightly garbled, the accents heavy. I wasn't sure what the students' native language was or if there was more than one.

As I read the lesson on the monitor, it was translated to each student. It automatically scrolled to the next step, stopping when I was to ask for feedback. There was no reason to have hired a credentialled teacher. There was no room for spontaneity. From the responses, there were students who could use a little extra help, but my hands were tied with the program.

After three months on the job, I was pleased to see real progress with some of the students, while others seemed unable to grasp the language. Exiting my room, I encountered another instructor. I had seen him before but there was little interaction among the instructors. Our schedules seemed to be arbitrary making me wonder if they offered round the clock classes.

"How are your little aliens today?" he asked.

"Just fine," I said, thinking how cruel of him to refer to people of another language like that. I walked past him.

"You don't like me calling them that, do you?"

I turned and looked back at him. "It doesn't seem very welcoming. They are trying to learn our language."

"Ha," he said. "What do you know about them?"

I wasn't going to get pulled into his prejudice and walked away.

"You probably think they came from across the border?

Despite my altruism, my curiosity was aroused. "Why do you say it like that?"

"Did you wonder why the entire course is all planned out for you?"

"I found that very...unchallenging," I admitted.

All our class conversations were scripted. One day I went off script and asked the students what they liked to do when they took time off. Their answers surprised me because their comments were about adult things, not childish. I hadn't realized my students were older. In turn they asked me the same question, and what did "y'all" mean. I explained about growing up in the South.

The next morning when I greeted them, "Good morning y'all." They responded including the "y'all." It made me feel connected, and I laughed.

* * *

When my six-month contract ended, I was thanked for my work. The administrator said I had done a good job, the client was satisfied, but there were no further lessons needed.

Later that week all hell broke loose. Every news station broadcast the arrival of UFO ships on Earth. It was like something out of an old sci-fi movie, only it was real. And the aliens spoke English. It made me think of *The Day the Earth Stood Still.*

The leader when interviewed said, "Good morning y'all."

TRUMPED

During the first deal, I watched the dealer with her green eyeshade and automatic shuffler and thought this was anything but a friendly game. I was here after reading a flyer posted in the apartment house where I moved recently. The ante was a quarter, and the bets came fast and furious.

I fanned my five cards and wondered if I had a poker face. No one knew me. And I didn't know how seriously they played poker.

Three hands dealt, and I was down to my last quarter. With eight players, we were looking at a two-dollar pot. No high stakes game. I couldn't believe the five cards I had been dealt. You didn't get a hand like this very often. Across the table Bill smirked. He didn't have a poker face. Everyone took a couple of cards. I kept the hand I was dealt. One by one, the players either raised the bet or folded. As the play rounded the table to me, I took out the key to my brand new car and slid it into the pot. "All in," I said.

"Call," someone said.

"Four of a kind," I crowed, and spread my cards on the table.

There were comments as everyone threw down their cards. I scooped the pile of quarters to me.

"Wait a minute. That's three Queens and a Jack. That's not four of a kind."

"Excuse me," I said. "You don't know Jack, he's transgendered."

That got a good laugh, and nobody demanded their quarters back. But from then on everyone made up a story about the hand they laid down. No longer did the old poker rules apply to our game, it was all about who could tell the best story with their cards

UNFORESEEN

Myrtle Johnson lived in Sea View Park and she had a secret. When she thought about it, she referred to it as the skeleton in her closet. But she never said that aloud.

After successful careers, she as a teacher and Harold an insurance agent with his own firm in Cedar Rapids, they moved west to a quiet mobile home park overlooking the Pacific Ocean. They were an odd looking couple, Myrtle stood six feet tall in her stocking feet, while Harold was a foot shorter. In retirement Myrtle volunteered at the local grammar school tutoring students with reading and spelling. Harold drove her to the school and arranged to circle back and pick her up promptly after school until one day he found himself helping a boy with math. From that point on, you could find both of them at the school tutoring children three afternoons a week. But in her seventy-third year, Myrtle broke her ankle and curtailed her excursions except for trips to the doctors and physical therapy. When Myrtle's ankle mended, she suggested that they drop into the school and resume their tutoring. They planned to go on Tuesday.

She awoke that Tuesday morning and prepared breakfast. The food was on the table and still no Harold, so she called again, then went to find him. She shook his shoulder. When he did not stir, she took his arm searching for a pulse.

"Oh Harold," she sighed. "Your breakfast is cold." Thinking that absurd, she added, "And so are you."

Picking up the phone she pressed nine, then one. Her finger hovered over the one button as she contemplated the consequences of reporting his death. It was only the seventeenth of the month, and their retirement checks weren't due for another week. It took both their checks to eke out their existence. On only her check, she couldn't make ends meet. She cancelled the call to consider her options.

Myrtle read up on what to do with a dead body. She walked up to the thrift store and purchased a used shower curtain and a garment bag. Carefully, she wrapped Harold in the shower curtain, and tucked him into the garment bag, pulling up Harold's legs so that he would fit. She tugged the package off the bed and dragged it into the closet. Everything that had been Harold's was moved there. Then she sealed the closet door with duct tape. She placed plug-in air fresheners in the room and in the hallway outside. After situating Harold, she moved her things into the guest bedroom.

She called the retirement office and asked what could be done about direct deposit for their checks and with a single signing of his name, the checks were directly deposited to their bank account. No longer would Myrtle have to wait for the mail and bring them to the bank to deposit them. This brought a relief she could not describe.

Myrtle told neighbors that Harold had a cold, the flu, took a fall, or wasn't feeling up to par. She developed quite a repertoire of insignificant banter about his ailments. Nothing too severe, nothing requiring an ambulance or a trip to the hospital. When she had to go out, she turned up the volume on the television and yelled as she went out the door, "Eat the sandwich I made for you," or "Don't just sit there all the time I'm gone."

Each month Myrtle wrote three checks; one to the trailer park, one to the power company and the third to the telephone company. Other than that, she walked to the grocery store and purchased her needs. She continued to go twice a week so that anyone watching wouldn't suspect her needs were less and less.

Despite her best attempts, an odor sometimes seeped under the door. She labored cleaning and airing out the house to little avail. She simmered cinnamon on the stove to counter it. Then things started to go wrong.

First, the refrigerator which they had purchased years before, suddenly could not maintain the freezer. She gave up on keeping anything frozen. Mostly she missed her nightly bowl of ice cream. In addition, the winter rains had dripped through the roof leaking in the kitchen and bathroom. Roof repairs were costly and needed.

On a walk through the neighborhood, she saw a for sale sign on a chest freezer in front of #93. She walked on but kept thinking about the freezer. She doubled back and asked about the price. Only fifty dollars? The man at #93 nodded. "We are going to move in with our son and daughter-in-law, and they don't need it." She agreed to give him a check for the full amount if he could deliver it to her carport. He agreed, and she hurried home to get her checkbook.

That very afternoon she moved several packing boxes of old school records out of the carport to make room for the freezer and tested the electrical outlet to make sure it was in working order. When Mr. #93 delivered the freezer, she gave him her check and thanked him, telling him she was looking forward to keeping two cartons of ice cream in it. He pocketed the check and headed home.

That night after midnight, she snuck quietly down the street to #55. Despite this being an over-fifty-five park, the lady in #55 had two young children living with her. And there in the driveway was a four-wheeled red wagon. Quietly Myrtle took the handle and led it home. Parking at the back of the trailer, she unlocked the master bedroom and pulled the duct tape off the closet door. Then she dropped to her knees.

"Harold, I'm so sorry that I was not able to give you the proper burial you deserved. Nor the fancy celebration of your life party. God knows you were deserving of all that, but do not begrudge me that I took the easier way and kept the retirement income. You knew how hard it was making ends meet. And now it's getting worse. The roof has a leak and the refrigerator is on its last legs. I got a lead on a used one and will try and make that work. But I can't have workers coming in here. I can't have people finding you like this. I figured it out. I got you a crypt. A good safe place for you. May the lord God have mercy on our souls. Amen."

Myrtle pulled the garment bag with Harold's remains through the bedroom to the back door, and onto the wagon. The wheels squeaked under the weight as she rolled back across the patio to the carport. A dog barked. An owl hooted. The moon filtered through the trees, but no neighbors lit their lights or called out. She opened the freezer lid and propped it open with a hammer. Then by only the light of the freezer, she tugged the bundle up out of the wagon, leaned it against the freezer, then shoved it over the rim. With a thud and a kerplunk, Harold rested on the bottom of the freezer, the hammer fell to the floor, and the lid banged shut.

"Oh Harold, I'm so sorry…tomorrow I will come out and play your favorite songs and we will have our own tribute to you…but now I need to return the wagon before anyone wakes up."

She slept through the next day.

* * *

Four years to the day after Harold did not wake, Myrtle lay unconscious on the kitchen floor. It took death three days to claim her. The trailer park manager came knocking when the rent was unpaid and found Myrtle. Neighbors reported that she was married but admitted they had not seen Harold for some time. Some had never seen him. When the police investigated they found Harold's remains in the freezer.

Their bodies were cremated and packaged for claiming by a family member – all being done on charity as the retirement checks stopped when their deaths were reported. Their accounts were empty. An attempt was made to find the next of kin.

An insurance policy came to light, which Harold arranged early in his career as an insurance agent. It was meant to help them, should one die before the other. The one-million-dollar policy would have provided amply for Myrtle's needs but it had been too many years since Harold had talked about that policy She'd forgotten. Because of the condition of Harold's remains, there was no way to verify that Harold had died from natural causes. The insurance company refused to pay on the claim.

UP IN FLAMES

Everything I knew about dragons lead me to believe they were dangerous and to be avoided. That is, if they existed. Most information pointed to the fact they did not, never had and never would be real—categorized with unicorns and gnomes.

But on an archeological trip to the rain forests of Brazil, I encountered a winged lizard that seemed to meet the criteria used to describe a dragon. At least movie screen dragons. And on a very small scale. This dragon was only eight inches in length and its wingspan no more than that. It hissed and crackled but spouted no fire, although it did seem to emit a slight Sulphur odor when it burped.

It seemed as fascinated with me as I was with it. I broke the rules and tucked it into my backpack. It could easily escape if it wanted to, back at camp it was still nestled in the pack.

I set it on a worktable and offered it some nuts, berries, leaves and water. What was its diet? Was it a known lizard? I searched for information but could find nothing that seemed to confirm its existence. Had I found a new species?

That thought excited me. I caged the lizard for the night planning to study it further.

The entire camp was awakened after midnight. There was a tremendous thundering and my tent shook. I flew outside and felt the air swirl around me. It wasn't a storm or an earthquake. A huge dragon hovered over the encampment, its talons clawed at the canvas. Its wings beat moving the air, canvas flapped, storage containers fell over. Then it screeched a noise that reverberated. My hands flew to cover my ears. The dragon blew a flame igniting my tent. Quickly it thrust its snout inside and removed the cage with the lizard.

I realized then what it was: a baby dragon. Horrified, I backed up taking cover In the trees. With the slightest pressure of the mother dragon's giant jaw, the cage splintered and fell away. My lizard clambered over the scales of the dragon's shoulder and clung behind its head. Again the beast roared, then threw a flamed breath at my tent, and lifted off. I cowered and watched in awe as the dragon majestically flew away.

All evidence I had of the little lizard was destroyed along with the tent and all my possessions. Sometimes in my dreams I hear that screech still.

WAITING

Cynthia Watson arrived early for her nine o'clock appointment with the gynecologist. She always scheduled her appointments for the first thing in the morning. Cynthia detested waiting.

She tapped the window when the receptionist did not immediately greet her.

"Cynthia Watson for Dr. Lopez," she said when the receptionist acknowledged her.

"Take a seat, you'll be called shortly."

Promptly at nine o'clock a smocked nurse stuck her head around the corner and called her name. Cynthia smiled, knowing she would be the first patient seen today, therefore, no waiting. After the customary weighing-in and verification of personal data including all medications, the nurse instructed Cynthia to remove her clothing and put on the baby blue gown. "Open in the back," she said exiting the exam room.

Cynthia picked up the folded paper gown. "Gown," she scoffed, remembering when it was soft cotton with tiny prints of flowers. "Our throw-away society," she muttered as she disrobed and unfolded the gown being careful not to rip it. After tying the single set of strings at the back of her neck, she backed up and sat on the tissue paper-covered exam table. "Like a piece of meat at the butcher's," she mused. With even the slightest movement, the various papers crinkled and crackled. Scooting backward, the paper beneath her ripped. She glanced at her watch. It was nineteen minutes after the hour. She took a deep breath, and when she exhaled, a slight sound of displeasure erupted. "Hurumph!"

Cynthia began tapping her fingers and watching the clock. One sure result of this would be her heightened blood pressure readings which that cause Doctor Lopez to launch into her speech about high blood pressure, stroke and stress. *Why can't we just start the appointment on time?* Cynthia wanted to say. Previous attempts to do so had resulted in long diatribes about other patients and emergency C-sections and on and on. Cynthia took another deep breath. *That's why they get your clothes off you right away,* she thought. *So you won't go out and ask what is taking so long. I could put on my clothes. I could leave and reschedule.* She was thinking of her options when there was a knock at the door.

"Ready," Cynthia called out. *Did they think anyone took that long to take their clothes off? Or what did they think she was doing?*

The door opened, and there stood the smocked nurse who had ushered her into the room. "Sorry," she said, "but there has been an emergency at the hospital, and Doctor Lopez has been detained."

"How long?" Cynthia asked in an exaggerated whine.

"She is on her way here, fifteen minutes tops," the nurse said.

"Okay," Cynthia said. When the nurse left, Cynthia

spied her bag on the floor. It was so much more than just a purse to carry her wallet and cell phone. It was a large blue canvas carry-all, big enough to hold her current needlework project and small purchases. Cynthia decided to use this time to clean out her purse. When she looked inside, she remembered shopping the day before. At Doodle-Bugs she bought scissors and sequins from the fifty percent-off-table. She laid the items on the exam table. There were three pairs of specialty scissors: one cut a rounded scalloped edge, another an exaggerated zig-zag edge and the last was a pair of pattern scissors, whatever that meant. She set out a small box of sequins, four ounces of rainbow colors all the same size and shape. At the bottom of the bag was a tube of glue perfect for adhering the sequins to any fabric. The last two words echoed in Cynthia's mind. *Any fabric?* Reacting quickly, she pulled off the gown and laid it on the exam table. Using the glue, she began to fasten a row of blue sequins across the gown. A line of red sequins marched out beneath the blue ones, and then a row of green. Without hesitating, she affixed a straight-line perpendicular to the horizontal ones using green sequins down the gown. At the lower edge of this line, she glued a tight triangle of silver sequins. She stood back and admired her work. *Not bad.* Testing the first sequins, she found that they were solidly attached. *That was quick.* She sorted out gold sequins and pasted them in twin circles above the horizontal rows. "Ha ha," she laughed.

Finally, she picked up the scallop-edged scissors and cut along the hem of the gown, shearing off a good three inches. Using the next pair of scissors, she zig-zag trimmed the edges of the section she had removed.

"This'll make a nice belt," she said, and was about to adhere some sequins when there was another knock on the door.

"Just a sec," she called out and stashed her art supplies back into her bag and put on the gown. "Ready," she said.

The door opened and Dr. Lopez, followed by the smocked nurse and a contingent of student doctors entered the room. "Today, I have rounds with interns..." Dr. Lopez began, but stopped mid-sentence. Everyone stood looking wide-eyed at Cynthia Watson.

Cynthia Watson stood next to the exam table. Her gown was embellished with two circles of gold sequins where her breasts were, three rows of brightly colored sequins around her waist and a silver-sequined arrow pointing down to her pelvic area.

"Well, that's a different look," Dr. Lopez said, "and I'm sure the interns will appreciate the road map. Will you take your place on the exam table?"

Cynthia climbed up on the exam table and lay down. She giggled, while visions of products for waiting patients to decorate their gowns danced in her head.

WHAT NOT

I waved across the restaurant to my friend, Bob. He raised his arm to signal back and jostled a passing waitress. I watched as her tray filled with glasses tipped, then crashed to the floor. The poor waitress bent to clear it under the scrutiny of the lunchtime crowd. Bob ducked out of view. The sound of glass breaking puts my nerves on edge and brought back a painful memory.

My mother had a what-not shelf that hung on the living room wall behind my dad's big overstuffed chair. Even as I think of this I ask myself, a what-not shelf? That's what she called it. It was a three-tiered wooden display, with intricately turned dowels between the shelves and railings. On the first day of each month she dusted and cleaned the display, setting aside her prized baubles. On the shelves were eleven small blown-glass figurines which she had acquired during her childhood. Each birthday her aunt would fashion one and mail it to her. It arrived in a wooden box, wrapped in yards of cloth. Her mother (my grandmother) made her a dress from the fabric, the figurine sat atop her dresser.

Mother explained that her Aunt Grace, an artist and glass blower, created them, one for each birthday. Unfortunately she died in a traffic accident before my mother was twelve, thus only the eleven.

These glass ornaments were of immense curiosity to me, but I was forbidden to touch them. Once mother took down the bird cage in which a tiny glass bird swung on a perch all within the cage. She held it gently in her hands and let me examine it. She explained how Aunt Grace had made the bird which was as small as the tip of my pinkie. Then she made the swing, and fashioned the birdcage enclosing them. The whole figurine was no bigger than four inches tall and as light as air. Sunlight glinted off the glass casting prismatic rays on the walls of the room. I marveled at each of the intricate but delicate figurines.

In addition to the bird cage, there was a ballerina twilling on her toes, an elephant, a tiger, and a beehive with a bee, no bigger than a kernel of popcorn. The giraffe was the largest of them, standing nearly seven inches tall, his long thin neck so delicate, not even as big around as my little finger. In total, they weighed less than a pound.

I never touched the shelf or the figurines, even when I was alone in the house. I wanted to, but I never did.

One day when I was a teenager, my mother called from the kitchen to come set the table for dinner. I said, "No, not now. I'm reading."

She said, "Young lady, you have five minutes to get in here and set the table."

I knew I was too old to throw a tantrum. I was old enough to know that I shouldn't have said what I said.

She stormed into the room when I missed the deadline. She towered over me, hands on her hips as I sat curled in my father's chair. "Charlene, you will come set the table. Now."

"All right," I said but as I stood, I tossed my book into the air.

Even as it left my hands, I realized where it would go. I held my breath and watched as the book nicked the corner of the what-not shelf. The display lurched just a little to the left.

I looked to mother, relieved that nothing happened, thoroughly regretting my actions.

As I watched, her expression changed from anger to fright. Her eyes widened, and she clenched her jaw. Her mouth opened in a perfect "O."

The silence in the room was broken by the tinkling of glass as each figurine slid off the shelf and shattered on the hardwood floor. She dropped to her knees inspecting the glass shards, like an emergency worker sorting through rubble looking for survivors. I watched in horror, then her breath caught.

Through my tears I saw her cradle the bird. The cage and the perch were gone, but the bird remained intact. She carefully nestled it into the pocket of her apron, and before she could say anything, I raced to the kitchen to set the table.

THE LAST MATH CLASS

"The number of males is five more than three times the number of females. If the total number of students is 73, how many of each gender are in the classroom?"

The words marched across the page. I read them over and over again. I looked around, it was unlike this classroom where the females outnumbered the males. And the only viable males, as far as potential boyfriends, were three. And they were all spoken for by long haired blondes in cheerleader outfits. I sighed.

"Five more minutes," the teacher called out.

Was he watching me? Did he see the beads of sweat forming on my brow?

I know how to work this problem...males would be 3x+5, m+f=73. Seventy-three in a classroom? That would be like a zoo. I looked around. There were seven rows of nine desks each. That was sixty-three. So, I guess another ten wasn't such a reach.

The last line in these word problems is always the killer. *How many of each gender are in the classroom?* See, it didn't account for the instructor or the instructor and an aide. And this is 2019; what about the transgendered? Fluid or non-declared? There was no right or wrong answer. If they had asked how many male students and female students maybe we could get close to the answer they were looking for.

The timer on the instructor's desk jingled like a wind-up alarm clock which is exactly what it was.

I looked down at my paper. Other than the doodle of "Dave" in the lower right hand corner, I had nothing more than my weak attempt at the algebraic formula.

"Make sure your name is on the paper and pass it forward."

I was about to write my name, but decided the lacy lettered Dave would suffice and passed it to the student in front of me. He smirked when he looked at it.

When all the papers were safely in the teacher's hands, he asked, "How many had seventeen for the number of females?" I watched as students checked left and right before they shot their hands up. Still their hands went only halfway up, tentatively.

"And the number of males would be?" he asked.

Again the students checked left and right as if no one would venture without reassurance from their peers, but a few were bent head down over paper scratching out the subtraction.

"Fifty-five," someone shouted.

"Fifty-six," I corrected. I can do simple subtraction, seventeen from seventy-three would be fifty-six, not fifty-five.

"You're right," he beamed at the class like we had solved some major world problem.

At least now, I had that smile for the right answer even though there was no paper in the pile with my name on it. If I was lucky I would get the grade anyway.

Truth was, this algebra was over my head. At home I would have pulled seventy three pennies out of the family piggy bank and laid them out to figure the answer that way. But he always wanted to see your work. I thought of sending him a photo of the pennies on the table.

The midterm grades came back, and I got another D. "I don't get it, I said to him. "Can you explain how this works another way?"

He patted my hand and looked away. "Tell you what, how about you earn extra credit by decorating my bulletin boards?"

And that was how I got the C in Algebra, my last math class. After all, I was an art major. His classroom had the best bulletin boards in the school.

Made in the USA
Middletown, DE
13 April 2022